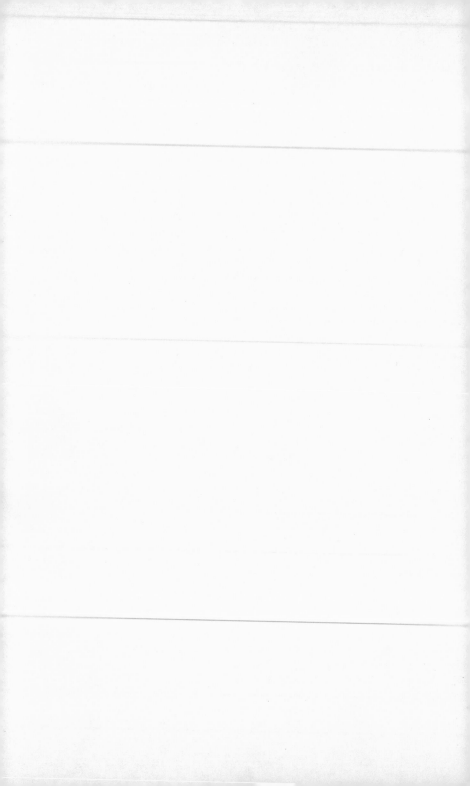

Seaward Born

LEA WAIT

Margaret K. McElderry Books
New York   London   Toronto   Sydney   Singapore

The author and publisher thank the following for permission to reprint the copyrighted material listed below. Every effort has been made to locate all persons having any rights or interests in the material published here. Any existing rights not here acknowledged will, if the author or publisher is notified, be duly acknowledged in future editions of this book.

Dover Publications, Inc., for excerpts from "The Farmington Canal Song," "The Hunting of the Wren," and "Old Pod-Auger Times" from *Folk Songs of New England,* collected and edited by Eloise Hubbard Linscott, copyright © 1939 by The Macmillan Company. Copyright © 1962, 1990 by The Shoe String Press, Inc. Copyright © 1993, Dover Publications, Inc. All rights reserved. Reprinted by permission.

Mystic Seaport Museum, Inc., for excerpts from "Blow the Man Down," "Blow, Ye Winds," "Across the Western Ocean," "Leave Her, Johnny, Leave Her," "The Sailor's Way," and "Home, Dearie, Home" from *Shanties from the Seven Seas,* collected by Stan Hugill, copyright © 1996 by Mystic Seaport Museum. Reprinted by permission.

University of Georgia Press for excerpts from "Until I Die," "When My Lord Calls Me I Must Go," "May Be the Las' Time I Don't Know," "Pay Me My Money Down," and "Wake Up Buddy" from *Slave Songs of the Georgia Sea Islands* by Lydia Parrish, copyright © 1942 by Lydia Parrish, 1969 by Maxfield Parrish Jr. Copyright © 1992 by Brown Thrasher Books, University of Georgia Press.

MARGARET K. MCELDERRY BOOKS
An imprint of Simon & Schuster Children's Publishing Division
1230 Avenue of the Americas, New York, New York 10020

Book design by Ann Sullivan
The text for this book is set in Goudy
Printed in the United States of America
2 4 6 8 10 9 7 5 3 1

Library of Congress Cataloging-in-Publication Data
Wait, Lea.
Seaward born / Eleanor Wait.
p. cm.
Summary: In 1805, a thirteen-year-old slave and his friend make a dangerous escape from Charleston, S.C., and stow away to head north toward freedom.
ISBN 0-689-84719-X
[I. Slavery—Fiction. 2. Runaway slaves—Fiction. 3. Stowaways—Fiction.
4. Sailing—Fiction.] I. Title.
PZ7.W1319 Se 2003
[Fic]—dc21   2001059026

FIRST
F
EDITION

For
my granddaughters,
Vanessa and Samantha Childs;

Nina DeGraff, Elizabeth Park, Diane Roehm,
Sherie Schmauder, and Emma Stephenson,
who listened and encouraged; and

Emma Dryden,
who has everything an excellent editor needs:
faith, intelligence, insight, and patience

Chapter 1

Dum spiro, spero ("While I breathe, I hope").
—state motto of South Carolina

*W*hy did the mistress want to see him?

Never in all the thirteen years Michael had lived in the slave quarters of the big house on Tradd Street had Mrs. Lautrec asked for him.

Had she sold him? Was she sending him to her son's plantation, Sotherfield, to sweat in the rice fields?

The questions echoed through Michael's head. He stopped swabbing the floor and looked out from the highest arcade of Saint Michael's Church, far above the red rooftops of Charleston. Mrs. Lautrec sent him to the church every morning to help Mr. Fitzhugh, the sexton. Swabbing the steeple balconies was his favorite task. Usually the sight of the vessels below him in the harbor was enough to let him forget the past months.

Early-spring breezes caught strands of his long, dark hair, worn, as a seaman's would be, tied with an eel-skin thong at the back of his neck. Michael moved to the railing.

He could see all of Charleston, not just from the Cooper River to the Ashley River, but way out to the islands, where Papa had taught him fishing and the ways of the waters, and to the sea beyond. Michael blinked away tears. Papa had drowned in last September's terrible hurricane. The swelling cargo of rice filling the ship *Concord* had burst the vessel's seams open and taken everyone aboard down with it. That same day Mama had been crushed when high gales knocked the chimney of Mrs. Lautrec's house through the roof. In one day that storm had taken both his parents.

He reached into his pocket and took out the small, smooth wooden fishing boat Papa had carved for him when he was small. "Every boy, no matter he be a slave, should have a toy," Papa had said. And what Michael had wanted more than anything else, even then, was a boat. He had played with that boat constantly until he was old enough to know toys were only for little children, and had hidden it under his straw-filled pallet. After Mama's and Papa's deaths he thought of it again. It comforted him to feel the smooth wood under his fingers; it made Papa and Mama and the days when he had been a child seem closer. It reminded him that he had been loved.

Michael looked out again at the harbor. How could anyone live without being close to the sea? Masted vessels filled the harbor, their sails like the great wings of angels, carrying people safely from one shore to another. Tall ships under sail had the power to take you to other worlds. Most days the sight of them brought him hope. Today it reminded him of what else he could lose.

"Boy! Come down here this minute! There are other chores to be done!"

It was Mr. Fitzhugh. Michael shoved the boat back in his pocket and picked up the bucket of dirty water and the mop. Mama would have been proud of him, keeping his namesake clean for the Lord. He took one last look seaward and then scrambled down the steep stairs, slipping on the damp steps and spilling some of the dirty water from the pail as he came.

What did the mistress want with him? Sirrah, the cook who had replaced Mama, had said Mrs. Lautrec wanted to speak with him after dinner. The waiting would make for a long afternoon.

Chapter 2

Tomorrow's sun will sure to shine,
Turn, sinner, turn O!

—from "Turn, Sinner, Turn O!" a South Carolina spiritual

*M*ichael swabbed the piazza and swept the garden yard and cut up onions and tomatoes for Sirrah's chicken pilau, but the hours passed slower than the honey she poured into her sweet potato pie. Finally Anny, Mrs. Lautrec's maid, brought word. Mrs. Lautrec wanted to see him in the parlor. Michael walked slowly to the front of the house.

"Michael, you're a good boy, and you're growing tall and strong. Your mama would have been proud of you."

"Yes, ma'am. Thank you, ma'am." As Mama had taught him, Michael looked down at his bare feet on the patterned carpet and not straight at Mrs. Lautrec. He didn't want to be thought uppity. Whatever Mrs. Lautrec was going to say would change his life. He knew it.

But he mustn't look afraid.

"Since your mama died, you've been helping Jim repair the damage that hurricane did to my house and garden. Now all has been restored, Michael, and I have no special need for you here."

Michael ground his fingernails into the palms of his hands as he forced himself to be still.

"Your mama was special to me, Michael. I think she would have liked you to stay close to where you grew up. But it's time you earned your keep and learned a skill. So I've decided to hire you out."

He looked down at the tiny, gray-haired woman who owned him, and then down at the floor again, quickly, in relief. "Yes, ma'am. Thank you, ma'am." Hiring out meant he'd be rented to another master who would pay Mrs. Lautrec for his work, but he'd still belong to her. Mrs. Lautrec was a good mistress. Michael had most feared being sold.

"Captain Arnold Linforth, down on Vanderhorst's Wharf, runs a lighter service, loading and unloading ship-rigged vessels too large to be docked. The captain tells me he could use a boy who knows a bit about the water and is willing to learn. Tomorrow you'll go there and give him this note." Mrs. Lautrec handed Michael a folded piece of paper. "You'll stay with him a year, and then I'll talk with him again. You do a good job for Captain Linforth, Michael. You can learn a lot from him."

"Thank you, ma'am." Michael bowed slightly. "Thank you very much!" He took a step toward the door but couldn't help turning and grinning at Mrs. Lautrec, even if it was uppity. "I'll work hard. I promise!"

He was going to work on the waterfront! Mrs. Lautrec could have sent him to a plantation. Or to be a gardener or a tanner or a barber or an ironsmith, or to learn any one of the hundreds of jobs for black men in Charleston. But she was sending him to the very place he longed to be—the waterfront.

He was going to work on a lighter! That would mean hefting and toting heavy boxes and bales and barrels, as Papa had done for years before he had been freed and earned enough to buy his own small fishing boat. A lighter was a sailing vessel in its own right and operated with a small crew. It was much bigger than fishing boats and canoes and pettiaugers. Lightermen learned the ropes as well as they knew the strain of heavy cargoes on their backs. The only job more exciting would be sailing a deepwater ship. This was a step along that road. He was going to work on the waterfront!

Chapter 3

All dem Mount Zion member, dey have many ups and downs;
But cross come or no come, for to hold out to the end.
Hold out to the end, hold out to the end,
It is my determination for to hold out to the end.
—from "Hold Out to the End," a South Carolina spiritual

That night Michael paced the garden in back of the big house on Tradd Street. Here he had sailed his boat in the cistern that collected water for the house and had listened to Mama tell stories of Africa. She had swept the hard, bare earth of Charleston as carefully as she had helped her mama smooth the land outside her home in Africa before she was captured by slavers. Here he had stood on a chair in the kitchen cutting up onions and okra for Mama's spicy gumbo. Here he had learned to use a hammer and a saw and helped Jim with repairs to the house. But tomorrow he would live near the wharf. Or maybe even *on* one!

Jim came out of the kitchen door they had painted blue to

ward off evil spirits. "You look as full of yourself as a dog's full of fleas," he said to Michael.

"Mrs. Lautrec chose the exact right job for me!" Michael spoke rapidly and kept walking. "Like she knew what was inside me; what I was dreamin'!"

"You don't want for folks to know your thoughts. Not white folks, for sure."

Michael slowed down. "That's what Mama always said. She said, 'Don't be showin' 'em what you know or what you think or what you feel. Person knows those things has power over you. Keep your power. Don't let it be stolen from you.'"

"Your mama right. White man can own your body. But he can't own your soul 'less you let him."

"Mrs. Lautrec saw me wantin' somethin' an' reached out and got it for me."

"Boy, she didn't get *nothin'* for you. You got to get your life for yourself. Don't be trustin' the future. Today life may look fine, but you not the one makin' the decisions. White folks is. Sure be nice when they decisions be what you want. Not so nice when they not."

Michael stopped. "Mistress be sendin' you back to Sotherfield?" Jim belonged to Master Harry, Mrs. Lautrec's son, owner of the family rice plantation. Jim was in Charleston now only because his carpentry skills had been needed at the city house.

"In the mornin'. You goin' to the wharves; I goin' to the fields."

"And Anny?" Jim and Anny had grown close during the winter.

"I love that woman like my life. But she be here and I be

there. Sundays, mebbe, I can get a ride sometimes. Folks borrow Master Harry's pettiauger an' ask for a pass so they can come to Charleston. For church, you know." Jim winked at Michael. "I 'spect I's gonna get awful religious right soon now. I feels it comin' on."

"Then I be seein' you and Anny, sometimes, Sundays."

"I 'spect so, Michael. Not all times. But there be ways. As long as Anny's in Charleston, then I be findin' 'em."

Anny stood in the blue doorway. She looked at them both. "Gonna be real quiet round here tomorrow."

Jim went over and put his arm around her. "Don't you be worryin', girl. You ain't seen the end of me. Or of Michael neither, I 'spect."

Michael's joy was too great for him to feel their sorrow. He headed for the room he shared with Jim and Sam over the carriage house. If he could sleep some, morning would come faster.

He sat on his pallet and held his small boat close. "Papa, my dream be comin' true! I'm goin' to work on the waterfront. I'm goin' to learn the seas, jus' like you."

Chapter 4

Do come a-long, do let us go,
Do come a-long, do let us go,
Jesus sittin' on de waterside.

—from "Jesus on the Waterside," a South Carolina spiritual

Vanderhorst's Wharf was in the midst of Charleston's water-front. There black women from the plantations unloaded vegetables or flowers they had grown, or brooms or pottery they had made on their own time, after tasks for their masters had been finished. They sold their wares to black Charleston women, who in turn sold the goods on the docks or in near-by streets. Cooks sold extra cakes or breads or the crisp sweet benne wafers made with sesame seeds that were part of the African heritage of Charleston.

Men cried out their goods or services too. Oystermen and fishermen, like Papa had been, sold fresh seafood on the wharves or streets nearby. Barbers set up shop on street corners. Blacksmiths and coopers and tailors worked close to the wharves.

Shop owners were white folks; street merchants in Charleston were black. Most black folks were slaves, working for their master or on their own time, but there were a few who had bought their freedom or been freed by their master in thanks for some service.

Michael sat with his back against the side of Captain Linforth's office, watching the bustling wharf. Inside, Captain Linforth stood behind a high cedar desk taking orders from ships' captains and mates who needed help loading or unloading their ships. *His inkwell must be the biggest in Charleston, and his pen the busiest,* Michael thought. Linforth's lightermen included four young men he had hired, like Michael, and another four he owned. They were seldom without duties.

Beginning before dawn, Michael had helped unload a ship full of mahogany logs ordered from Honduras by a Charleston cabinetmaker. Under the direction of Cudjoe, the slave who was the captain's assistant and lighter pilot, he had helped sail Captain Linforth's lighter, the *Clarissa,* to where the ship was anchored. For six hours they had passed the heavy logs up out of the cargo hold, hoisted them high above the ship's deck, and then lowered them onto the lighter. After filling the lighter, the men had sailed back to the wharf, where they unloaded the logs and placed them on a wagon. It had taken thirteen wagonloads to deliver all the logs to King Street.

During his first few weeks working for Captain Linforth, Michael found his back and arms and thighs had ached, and the skin on his hands had bled from the salt water and the ropes. Now, four months later, his muscles were stronger and the skin on his hands was thick and callused. Michael was proud of those calluses. His hands were now the hands of a man. A lighterman.

Every day he was trusted more to set the rigging and handle the sails at the captain's or Cudjoe's directions. He knew the difference between a sheet anchor, a spare anchor, a bower anchor, a stream anchor, and a kedge. He knew how to strap a block so the rope lay even. He could splice a rope. He could tie a stopper knot or a shroud knot or a bowline without having to be told which knot should be tied where.

Michael took a deep breath of the salt air, full of the smells of the tides and the marshes where the ocean met the shore, and hoped for a breeze. July heat was heavy. The wharf was wet with sweat.

He and Cudjoe were mending a sail. The heavy canvas, stiff with salt spray, was spread between them as they sewed on patches with large needles and waxed sail twine. Michael pulled off his shirt. His hire badge, the copper medallion that hung on a chain around his neck to identify him, gleamed on his chest: #76, PORTER, CHARLESTON, 1805. He couldn't read it, but he knew what it said. Someday maybe he would have a medallion like Papa had worn. The kind that read, FREE MAN. Papa's father had owned him, but his will had given Papa his freedom. Papa had been saving money from the fish he sold to buy Michael from Mrs. Lautrec. More than anything, Papa had wanted Michael to be free. He always said, "You think toward freedom. You see a possibility, you take it."

"Boy, stop dreaming. We got to get these sails finished," admonished Cudjoe. "Captain'll have you back inside polishing brass in front of him if these sails ain't done right and fast." Cudjoe was in charge when he was needed, but Captain Linforth made sure he had his share of simple work to do too. Wouldn't want a slave to begin thinking he was better than the others. The captain was a fair man, but he expected full work from his people. Once he had made Michael start a task over from the beginning because he hadn't completed it exactly right.

"When I be young like you, boy, I be lookin' too," Cudjoe went on in a softer voice. "Lookin' at the girls and lookin' at the ships and dreamin' big dreams."

It was hard to believe Cudjoe had ever been young. His hair was gray, his face was lined, and his skin was the texture of the canvas they were sewing—rough and hard. Marked by years of work in the sun on wharves and the sea.

"Did you really work on a coaster?" Coasters were small sailing vessels that carried passengers and goods between coastal cities. They had small crews and short layovers. Michael concentrated on the sail he was stitching. He knew Captain Linforth would check every stitch to make sure they were even. If wind could find a space between stitches, it could tear a sail, endangering a vessel and its cargo.

"I did. Many times," Cudjoe answered proudly. "Been to Norfolk an' Williamsburg, an' even Philadelphia."

"Philadelphia! That be far north!"

"There be farther. There be New York an' Providence an' Boston an' Portland. Now bein' north means somethin'. I hear African folks in Philadelphia be free now. When I be there, black folks in Philadelphia was same as here. But there wasn't near as many of us up north as in Charleston."

Most of the people on the docks were black—rivermen, porters, maids and cooks and drivers from the big houses, coopers delivering barrels, carpenters, smiths, and he and Cudjoe. More than half the people in Charleston were black.

"Who do the work in Philadelphia?"

"White folks does it," said Cudjoe. "Up north white folks tote and carry and get their hands in the dirt. They even be doin' pickup work."

"You foolin' me!" The worst job in Charleston was doing pickup work in the summer on one of the red horse-drawn scavenger carts. Men on the carts opened drains, picked up manure and rubbish, and cleaned out privies. The stench of horses was usual in a Charleston street in July. But the stench of the scavenger carts required shutters to be slammed shut for blocks around. Black men worked on the carts, of course. Michael couldn't imagine a place where white men would do such work.

"It be true, sure enough."

"Don't they be wantin' more black folks up there? To do such things?"

"It be different up north. Some of us there work for the white folks, like we does here, but they's not owned. They gets paid to be workin'. Black men on the waterfront or workin' at sea gets paid too. Not as much as white men do sometimes, but paid, just the same."

Papa, too, had told Michael that in the North black men could sign on as mariners, like white men. Sometimes Michael saw those black mariners from the North swaggering proudly near the Charleston docks, drinking at the grogshops and tippling sheds, telling elaborate yarns and sea stories.

He leaned toward Cudjoe. "Someday I goin' to sail. Not just sail in Charleston Harbor, but to sea. I be seein' those big northern places like Philadelphia. Maybe even London!"

Cudjoe harrumphed. "Not likely, boy. Charleston slaves be free to take pettiaugers to and from plantations or operate lighters in the harbor. Some black folks—like Captain Whithers's Samuel—even learn to pilot. Course, Samuel can't be called a pilot, 'cause he be black, but when Samuel on a ship, the white pilot can drink his rum and know the ship they're bringing into harbor will get here well enough."

Samuel was prized for his skills; but even Samuel wasn't permitted far outside Charleston Harbor.

"But you sailed to Philadelphia!"

"That happen before blacks in the North were free. No place to run to then. Today Charleston captains headin' north only use us when they got no white mariners to sign on. They're afeared of us takin' off, stealin' ourselves in those northern ports."

Michael's voice rose with excitement. "I wouldn't be runnin'. I'd just be sailin'. Provin' to myself I can do it!"

Cudjoe glanced around and lowered his voice to a whisper. "Don't be saying nothin' close to soundin' like you wantin' to leave Charleston, you hear, boy? Someone hears, you be in deep trouble. Whippin's not just for slaves that run. White folks might get to thinkin' you're prone to goin'. An' runnin' ain't easy. Most who run be caught. White folks has the power and the eyes, and they helps each other."

"Black folks help each other too."

"They be helpin' when they can, sure enough. But a free black man hidin' a runaway can be sold and made a slave himself. An' if a white captain be takin' a slave out of Charleston in his ship, then that captain won't be doin' no business in Charleston again."

Michael thought about that for a moment. "I've seen scars on folks that ran."

"And those folks you seein' be the lucky ones. Stealin' yourself and bein' caught means maybe death. At least a bad lashing. Thirty-nine strokes for the first time. After that, maybe losing an ear, or more." Cudjoe glanced down meaningfully. "A man can lose some parts of him that make him a man."

Michael shivered.

"It was done to men I knew. Este, down on the Wando, and Joseph, who hid out behind some cotton bales headed for Liverpool." He lowered his voice even further. "For talkin' as we are, we could be in for a whippin' and be put in jobs far from the sea. White folks know the sea's temptation. Our fathers and mothers came 'cross those waters. Always be some who'll want to cross back. Or follow that North Star to places like London or Boston, where Africans can make new lives."

"How far would a man have to go?" Michael couldn't help asking. "How far to be free?"

"Farther north you get to, the better. Farthest in these United States would be District of Maine. It be the north part of Massachusetts, before the north seas and Canada."

"I knows Maine!" Michael smiled at the memory. "Mistress had a fancy dinner party and Sam brung a whole barrel full of big green lobsters from the wharves. They was packed all around in sawdust. And ice. From Maine!"

He remembered the cruel-looking creatures Mama had

puzzled over cooking and then boiled like giant shrimp until they turned as red as summer sunset. But what he remembered best was the clear coolness of the ice. It numbed his fingers and tongue, and as it melted it chilled his whole mouth and throat. "That ice. I thought that ice be from a place like heaven. A place clear and cold."

Cudjoe looked at him. "You ever seen snow, boy?"

Michael nodded. "Couple of years back there was snow. Like little specks of soft white sand fallin' from the sky. Mama said it was tiny feathers from angels' wings. Then it disappeared."

"Well, I hear that Maine place has plenty of snow, in winter, anyway. That land be white with snow, and waters so filled with ice a man can walk across rivers, like Jesus done."

Michael listened in awe. "Rivers you can walk on? Land white with snow?"

"I've heard. Never seen it, but I've heard."

"Mebbe a story. Sounds too much like heaven to be real."

"You ask, then. You see vessels out of places like Boston and Portland and Wiscasset and Camden—those be Massachusetts and District of Maine places—you ask." Cudjoe looked at him closely. "But you ask quiet, you hear? Not when any white folks be near."

"I will." Michael moved his feet on the hot boards of the wharf so his soles wouldn't burn. A river of ice. A vessel that would take him to a river of ice, where everything was cool and clear.

"Tell you what. I knows a black mariner—Moses Smith— good man, out of Boston. He be free, usually workin' on a merchant ship. Couple times a year he come to Charleston. When he here, he be rummin' at the Lucky Bag. When next

17

I see him, I'll make him your acquaintance. He'll tell you 'bout that snow and ice. He knows."

"I'd be likin' that." Michael leaned back against the wooden slats of the building, looking out over the harbor. Schooners and pettiaugers and hot sun were reflected in the calm blue waters. He tried to imagine waters white with ice and snow. "I'd surely be likin' to meet that Moses Smith. I surely would."

Chapter 5

Let me tell you what is nat'rally de fac'
Who is on de Lord's side,
None o' God's chil'un nebber look back.
Who is on de Lord's side.

—from "Who Is on the Lord's Side?" a South Carolina spiritual

By October the heat and humidity of summer had subsided, so Michael could breathe easily as he worked, and his muscles pulled and pushed and toted and carried without hesitation. He could feel the winds and the waves and knew the ways the *Clarissa's* sails should be set and trimmed to let them catch harbor breezes. Even Cudjoe, who ran a tight vessel, nodded at Michael in approval. "Cap'n Linforth, you made a right good decision when you hired Michael," Cudjoe had said in Michael's hearing. "That boy is seaward born."

Michael woke with the light of dawn, not wishing to waste a moment of a Sunday at liberty. As he sat on the wharf and chewed a piece of bread he watched a blue heron fish in the shallow waters of low tide. The tall, slender bird stood absolutely still. Maybe not even breathing. Then, suddenly, his long neck swooped down into the water, and when his head emerged, he held a fish or small crab. That bird could tell you. You had to watch, and you had to wait, and then you had to act, to get what you wanted. Michael envied the heron its patience, but not its meal. He preferred his fish cooked.

After the heron departed in search of better prey, Michael skipped stones for a while, until the sun was high enough for people to be about. Then he went back to the room he shared with Captain Linforth's other men above the dock. He was the youngest of the eight, and the only one who had not spent Saturday night in a tippling shed. The snores and moans of the sleeping men filled the small room as Michael carefully put on his good white cotton shirt. Mama had made it for him, and the sleeves no longer covered his arms to his wrists. Soon it would be too tight to pull over his head and chest. But it was his good shirt and he wore it every Sunday. He tucked his boat into his pocket and he was ready.

He and Mama had always attended divine services at Saint Michael's, sitting on benches designated for slaves in the balcony overlooking the high-boxed cedar pews on the ground floor, where white families sat. Michael continued to attend church every week. Mrs. Lautrec would often look up at him from her pew in the center of the church and nod her approval. Anny made certain Mrs. Lautrec was settled before joining Michael and Sirrah and Sam on the benches.

After services Michael returned to Tradd Street, where he told Sam and the women about life on the waterfront— which vessels had arrived and which had left, which captains

20

were fair and which mistreated their crews—and heard the Lautrec family gossip. After dinner, unless Mrs. Lautrec had other needs, Michael and Anny went to hear one of the black preachers who spoke over in Charleston's Neck. Today Anny hoped Jim would be joining them there. She had been whispered word from a woman selling chickens from kitchen to kitchen that she had heard from a woman who knew a man from the plantation next to Sotherfield that this Sunday the Lautrec pettiauger would carry a full load of folks to the city for services, and Jim would be among them.

"Michael, boy, that shirt be way too small for you," Sirrah declared as she washed the dishes from their dinner of rice pie with chicken and stuffed tomatoes. At the Lautrec house slaves ate close to what Mrs. Lautrec ate. Michael missed that good food at Captain Linforth's, where plain rice and bread and fish were standard fare. Sirrah looked at the shirt again. "When I gets the time, I be makin' you a bigger one."

"Mama stitched this one."

"An' she made a right fine shirt for the boy you were. But you're gettin' to be a man. Keep that shirt to remember if you want, but you'll be needin' another to wear."

"Thank you, Sirrah."

"No trouble. I got no man or child of my own to sew for. Might as well keep you and Sam covered decent."

Sirrah wiped the table as Michael paced from one end to the other of the long kitchen that stretched from the main house to the slave quarters. "How long is Anny goin' to take?"

"Mistress be gettin' on and losin' strength. She be nappin' after her dinner every day now. Anny'll be here soon as she's sleepin'." Sirrah piled another dish on the stack to be dried.

"Heat was hard for the mistress this summer. She should have gone north like those friends of hers, the Dunlaps. They sail to Newport in summers. But no, Mrs. Lautrec say Charleston her home and she stayin' here." Sirrah shook her head. "Think of havin' the choice of where you're to live or bein' able to just take off and go someplace, knowin' you can be comin' back when you choose."

Anny appeared in the doorway. "Michael, you ready?" She ran her hand over her hair and took off her apron. "Sundays everythin' seemin' to take five times longer than other days."

"'Specially on Sundays when that man of yours be comin' to Charleston." Sirrah shooed Anny and Michael out the door. "Hope he be there. You give him a word from me and bring back the news."

Anny nodded and grabbed Michael's hand as they headed out of the house and toward the edges of town where Charleston's blacks gathered on Sunday.

Jim was there, sure enough, waiting for them and watching a black preacher lead several dozen people in a livelier version of Christian services than Anny and Michael had attended earlier at Saint Michael's. The sentiments were the same, but here the songs of joy and Christian love were accompanied by the rhythmic clapping and stomping of the congregation rather than by a pipe organ imported from England. The singers had spent the week hiding their emotions from their masters and even, for safety's sake, from themselves. Sundays were a day to let those feelings out and direct them toward the Lord.

Michael tapped his foot and smiled but followed Anny and Jim as they moved slowly away from the crowd. Today was the first Sunday Jim had been able to leave Sotherfield in several weeks. Michael half listened to Anny and Jim sharing how much they'd missed each other. Maybe he would visit Mama's grave and then try to beat the herons to some crabs for dinner.

"Jim, you lookin' fine, and I know Anny can hardly wait till I leave you two." He turned to go.

"Wait, Michael. I be needin' to talk with you. And Anny. There be thoughts in my head, and you be the two I can trust with 'em."

Michael and Anny exchanged questioning glances as Jim gestured for them to follow a path that led past sea myrtle bushes covered with soft mounds of pale yellow flowers into the marsh where the Ashley River met the land. A little way down, with no one nearby, they sat on the remains of an old wharf that broke up the sea of grasses. The dank smell of the dark marsh soil beneath their feet surrounded them like rotten eggs in a henhouse.

"Things are changin' for sure," Jim blurted out. "An' I be scared they be changin' us. Anny and me."

"What you sayin', Jim? Ain't nothin's goin' to change what we feel for each other."

"Mebbe not. But life can change where we are and when we can be together."

They were all silent, knowing that was true.

"Master Harry's not doin' well growin' rice. I heared other planters tellin' him to switch to cotton, like they be doin' now. But he's stubborn an' stays with the rice 'cause he knows it. He be owin' money. Told us times ain't good. He sold off Dan'l and his wife and children this week. Tried to keep them together, he said, but couldn't get the right offer. They went to three different families—two here in Carolina and one somewheres else. Anny, I couldn't bear it if you or I was sold far away so we couldn't be seein' each other."

"It won't be happenin', Jim. Mrs. Lautrec won't sell me, and you're a carpenter. You got a skill Master Harry can use." Anny made it all sound simple. "A skilled African is valuable."

"And would fetch a good price. Master have two other men who can build. There's no way of knowin' the future. 'Lessen you make that future what you needs it to be."

Jim sounded just like Papa. Papa had always said, "You see a possibility, you take it. You think toward freedom, boy. Promise me you'll do that. A fish you pull in as a free man tastes ten times sweeter than a fish you catch for a master."

Michael looked at Jim. "What you be sayin'? Black folks got no say in what they do or where they go. You told me that yourself 'fore you went back to Sotherfield."

"I did. But I be talkin' 'bout black folks who be owned. Slaves. Black folks who own themselves, they can do what they please."

"There ain't many of those, Jim, and you knows it. The price is too high," Anny said.

"I wasn't thinkin' of buyin' freedom."

"You were thinkin' of runnin'? Jim, don't talk about such things! Most all folks that run be caught. And what good would it be to me to love a dead man—or one livin' his life hidin' in swamps or wilderness?" Anny shook her head. "We got to be happy with what we got now and think of that. Not think of what we can't do nothin' about."

"But we could both go! Michael, you load and unload vessels every day, don't you?"

Michael nodded. "Mebbe a dozen a week, dependin'."

"And you know those brigs and ships well, don't you?"

"Inside an' out," Michael bragged.

"Well, then, you'd be knowin' every space a person could hide in one of them vessels."

Michael looked from Jim to Anny and back again. "I couldn't be doin' such a thing. I'm never alone. I'm with Captain Linforth's crew. And captains check for runaways. Any captain who 'lowed such a thing would be ruined in Charleston."

"But it happens."

"An' most who tries it gets caught. Three or four since I been on the waterfront."

"What happened to 'em?" asked Anny, reaching for Jim's hand. "Those who got caught?"

"One was run through with a sword an' dumped in the harbor. Others was lashed till they couldn't stand an' then sold away to the Alabama Territory." Michael spoke softly as he repeated the horrors. Alabama had opened up to cotton plantations, and traders were looking to buy groups of slaves, cheap, to clear the lands and live in the wilderness far from Carolina. Slaves sold between plantations near Charleston could still see family and friends. Slaves sold to Alabama were gone forever.

"But you don't know the ones who 'scaped! We can do it, Anny, I'm sure. You, too, Michael. You know vessels; you know men who work in the harbor. We could all leave. Get ourselves to a northern port where there ain't no slavery." He clutched Anny's hand. "My children and grandchildren ain't gonna be white folks' tools. They gonna be born in freedom."

Michael shook his head. "Even if we got north, there be slave catchers. Men who make money bringin' black folks back to their masters. We'd probably be caught or killed. Or both."

"Then we'd die makin' our own ways! Not waitin' for white folks to decide what to do with us." Jim looked hard at Michael. "You got to help us, Michael. You can go or stay. But you got to help Anny and me leave. Together."

Anny stood up. "I's scared, Jim. I can't go neither. And now you've made me afeared you'll try. Why can't we stay as we is? Why be changin' everythin'?"

"Michael?" Jim's voice was urgent.

Michael's hand went to the disk he wore around his neck. "I can't, Jim. Captain Linforth knew I be talkin' 'bout such things, he be makin' certain I never be hired again in Charleston Harbor." He got up before he could change his mind. "I couldn't stand not workin' on the waters. I can't help. I can't."

Michael left Anny crying in Jim's arms. He walked quickly along the narrow path through the grasses back to town. "I can't be helpin'. There be too much to lose."

He burst into a run and ran as fast as he could past the crowd near the preacher and toward the wharves.

Papa's voice repeated in his mind. "You see a possibility, you take it."

Well, this wasn't a possibility. This was crazy. This was dangerous. It wasn't fair of Jim to have asked him. They could be hurt. Or killed.

Jim would come around. He had to. He wouldn't run without Anny, and Anny wouldn't run. There was no reason for Michael to get involved.

No reason at all.

Chapter 6

Oh, one day as anoder, Hal-le-lu, Hal-le-lu!
When de ship is out a-sailin', Hal-le-lu-jah!
—from "Hallelu, Hallelu," a South Carolina spiritual

Michael's interest in Massachusetts and District of Maine places was now known on the waterfront, and was a matter of some concern, as Cudjoe had predicted. Cudjoe made a show of joking about it with the other men, telling them Michael was just a boy who thought heaven was full of ice. That way, he explained quietly to Michael, perhaps word would reach them about vessels from the north without anyone's taking Michael's interest as a threat. Africans who were interested in the north were all too common and all too dangerous. Their ideas might incite running or even rebellion. Either would upset the order of Charleston. But Michael was just a foolish young boy. No harm in being that.

Michael knew he shouldn't be seen asking questions. But today he'd finished his tasks and he'd heard a District of Maine vessel was in for repairs at Gadsden's Wharf. He hugged himself and walked faster. Even with the sun shining, January was cold. Today the air must be no more than fifty degrees.

He really wanted to see that brig. Just see it. Maybe talk with one of the seamen. He still dreamed of rivers of ice, although on days like today those rivers didn't sound as tempting as they had in high summer. Michael shivered. Spring couldn't come too soon.

Some said thirty fully loaded ships could be docked at Gadsden's Wharf, even at low tide. But today there were only seven and most were not fully loaded.

Michael looked at the vessels. Better to listen and find out for yourself and not be remembered. There was only one brig that looked in need of repair. There was damage to her stern, and she was listing to starboard. As he looked a young white seaman in square-toed brown leather shoes and a heavy blue sea jacket came up and stood next to him on the dock. "Run aground on Charleston Bar, they say. Captain didn't know the harbor. Tight little brig otherwise."

Michael nodded. Wouldn't be the first vessel to hit the bar. The young man's voice didn't sound like one from Carolina. "Where's it from, do you know?" Michael ventured softly. There was no one else around, and this seaman was young and from the North. He might not question Michael's interest.

"Says right there, clear as can be. *Fame*, out of Wiscasset, District of Maine."

Michael looked at the letters. He couldn't read them, but he tried to remember their shapes so he'd recognize them again.

"Which part be sayin' 'Maine'?" he asked daringly. He could be lashed for trying to learn to read.

"The last part, starting with that big letter that looks like two people bowing to each other. That's an M." The boy grinned proudly. "I went to school for two years before going to sea. I know my letters."

"You be sailin' on that Maine brig?"

"Nah. I'm out of Baltimore. We shipped to Providence for rum, sneaked into the islands despite the English, and traded for molasses. We're headed home. Ran into some heavy winds, and the captain decided to stop in Charleston to sit them out. I'm off the *Sally*. She's docked over there." He pointed to a yellow brig with red stripes on the far side of the wharf.

Michael stared at the M so he'd be sure to remember it. But he didn't want to stand too long with this white boy. In some waterside grog shops free black and white seamen mingled; men who knew one another from Charleston talked. But for a slave to be seen with a northern white boy looking at a northern ship was foolhardy. Especially for a slave known to be interested in northern ports.

Michael turned to head off the wharf.

The white boy started to follow him, but Michael walked faster and the boy stopped.

That boy don't know, Michael decided. *Don't know the difference between a black lighterman who's a slave in Charleston and a white boy who's a seaman from Baltimore. Don't know the dangers in talking.*

But now Michael knew what an M was, that meant "Maine."

Chapter 7

Hey, buddy
It's hard but it's fair
You had a good home
But you wouldn't stay there.

—from a Sea Islands work song

The Lucky Bag was crowded. Smells of grog and tobacco and men who knew seawater more than bathwater filled the small tippling shed, a place where black men, slave or free, bought spirits. Sharp odors and smoke circled above the heads of the men, filling the space to the low ceiling. Shadows from tallow candles in tin sconces on the walls and an iron chandelier hanging close to the center of the room made the faces of the black men fade into the crowd and the smoke. The sound of different voices bragging about exploits, telling yarns, and remembering families far away filled the room.

Michael took a deep breath of fresh outside air and

stepped in. Captain Linforth had written permissions that allowed all the adult slaves working for him to buy spirits. As long as they were sober enough to work in the morning he felt their time and any coins they had were theirs to spend. Michael would rather spend his coins on benne wafers and fishing line. But today Cudjoe had sent word to join him. Michael was too young to drink, even with his owner's permission, but his height let him mix with the older men without comment.

Cudjoe saw him first.

"Michael! Boy! Here, in the corner!"

Michael turned. Cudjoe was sitting with another man. Michael made his way through the crowd toward them.

"He's here! Just as I told you." Cudjoe pointed at the man seated next to him.

The man was about Michael's height, stocky, and perhaps Papa's age. His thick black hair was beginning to gray. He wore a heavy blue jacket with brass buttons and the wide, tar-stained trousers of a sailor, as did most men in the Lucky Bag.

"It's Moses Smith, from Boston. Didn't I say he'd be comin' here soon?" Cudjoe said.

Michael pulled over a stool so he could join them. "Pleased to be meetin' you." He reached out to shake Smith's hand. The hand was hard with years of pulling ropes at sea, and the grip was firm.

"Boy here's name is Michael. He be new at seafarin', but he be learnin' fast. His papa and mama are both gone, and he's hired out to Captain Linforth. I've worked with him for near a year now."

Smith nodded. "Pleased to meet you, Michael. If Cudjoe

says you're a good man, then I know it to be true. Cudjoe and I, we've known each other too many years. Right?"

Cudjoe laughed and raised his half-empty tankard of grog. "Right, for sure. We know each other from back when we were young men. I was sailin' on a coaster, and Moses here, he worked the ports too."

"We both had a taste for rum and a taste for talk, and being of the same color meant we found the same places welcoming us in ports."

"True enough. Now, Michael's been thinkin' about the North and wanting to know 'bout it. I figured you could tell him, true."

Moses Smith glanced around quickly. "Why are you wanting to know, boy? You're hired out, so you belong to some white master. He'll not be wanting you too interested in the North."

Cudjoe put his hand on his friend's arm. "It's too noisy in here, Moses, for anyone to see or hear. Most have had grog enough not to care. The boy's not plannin' on runnin'. He just wants to be knowin' what's at the northern end of this country we're livin' in."

Moses seemed satisfied with the answer. He leaned back a little. "I live in Boston, which is a grand, large city. Larger than Charleston, I think. Got a wife and three daughters there. Fine girls. Youngest is about your age, I'd guess. No man can own another in Massachusetts now, so there are a number of us African folks there. Some men work on the land or have trades, like being a cooper or a smith and so on. Women work in the houses of white folks, but in Boston they get paid to do it. A good number of us work the seas."

"Like here in Charleston?"

Moses looked around him. "Not like Charleston. Here there are many more Africans than there are in Massachusetts. And here most dark faces are property. In Massachusetts we're free people. A man can succeed, too. Some Africans are captains now, in Massachusetts, and have their own vessels. It isn't easy being black where most folks are white. But being free is a whole lot better than not."

That's what Papa had said, thought Michael. "Maine be like that, too?" he asked, thinking of the damaged brig and the M like two men bowing.

"Maine's but a district of Massachusetts—same laws, same governor, but wilderness, mostly, up on the frontier, north, near Canada. There are some black folks there, but not as many as in Boston."

"An' there be ice in Boston?"

Smith laughed and clapped Michael on the shoulder. "To be sure, boy. Lots of ice. October to March, for sure, and sometimes later. And snow. Snow so the land and the houses and the roads and the trees are covered with it, like a feather blanket from God."

"An' Maine?"

"If you're wanting ice and snow, Michael, Maine is the very place to think of. They have even more ice and snow than we have in Boston. And fewer roads to dig out. Most people in Maine live near the water. Some make their living from the seas; some farm or lumber or provide services for the others. Fishing is important in Maine and up along the coast to the Grand Banks of Canada. So many cod in those waters a vessel can sink from the weight of them. Massachusetts fishermen head for the Banks when they want full ships. Seas there are so full of fish you could walk across the ocean on their backs."

Cudjoe grinned. "Now, don't be tellin' this boy stories, Moses. He'll be believin' they're real as that ice and snow you're talkin' 'bout."

"Don't know it ain't true. There are fish for the world on those Canada Banks."

"What're you in Charleston for this trip, Moses?" Michael thought of those seas of fish and that ice. Places far from the world he lived in.

"I'm here this trip on a packet, the *Verity*, docked over to Cochran's Wharf. Brought some passengers down from Newport and New York for the social season. Some northerners don't like that ice and snow as much as you do, Michael. We're laying over here a week or so, and then we'll be heading back up the coast. The captain advertised in the *Charleston Times* for passengers and parcels, and we'll take what we can back north after a week of March sunshine and breathing the wisteria and dogwood blossoms."

"Not near as many ships here from New England as most years, Moses. Usually in springtime we be seein' numbers of ships from Providence and Boston. And"—Cudjoe looked over at Michael—"from that District of Maine."

"You heard the English and the French are fighting again?"

"They always be doin' that."

"True enough. Well, the English navy's been in want of sailors, and these past six months they've been stopping vessels, American vessels, just off the coast and impressing the seamen."

"Impressin' them?" Michael had heard the word *impressing* before but didn't know its meaning.

"Making them official British navy seamen, whether they're wanting to change countries or not. American captains have been finding other routes or staying close to port so they don't lose their crews."

"Them English tormented the United States enough in the past. Seems like they'd leave us alone." Cudjoe took another gulp from his newly refilled glass.

"But they're doing it. Here and in other places too, I've heard. They're angry that American ships still trade with the West Indies when England doesn't want them to. So they stop ships in southern waters more than in northern."

"Your captain came," Michael pointed out.

"It's a small packet, the *Verity*. We stayed close to land. Those passengers coming for the fancy parties in Charleston were willing to pay well." Moses rubbed his thumb and forefinger together as though he held coins. "And Captain Surridge does like trips to Charleston. He has a special hankering for shrimp pie and rice." He laughed to himself.

"How big a crew you be carryin'?"

"There's nine of us, plus the captain. Good men from Boston and Providence and Connecticut. I've sailed with most before. Not all friendly, but only two to watch out for. Ezra Lean is the most trouble. He's a white man with a mean scar on his face and a mean temper. And this trip his friend Ben Trader is sailing with us. Nasty, they are, especially to me and to our cook, Jack Strong, who's African too. Keep joking how they'll sell us both and make their fortunes."

Cudjoe shook his head. "You be careful, Moses," he counseled. "There be white men doin' just that. Boston is far away. Here in Charleston you be just one more African body."

"Such men are in Boston, too, preying on free black folks. But Captain Surridge is a fair man. He does not take notice of color, so long as work is well done. He's hired me and other African mariners before. Lean and Trader just better stay clear."

"Hope so, Moses, hope so. Getting' back to Boston's best for you. There be too few free men in Charleston. And too many white men lookin' to put dollars not rightfully earned in their pockets." Cudjoe was serious.

"I'm getting old, my friend. Too old to fetch a high price. Why, those slavers are looking for young men—like your Michael, here. They're the ones planters will pay big dollars for. Right, Michael? Prime flesh, right here."

The older men laughed as Michael shrank back from their teasing. Being sold was something he didn't want to think of. Not even to joke. That Moses, he was from the North. He couldn't really know.

In Charleston there were few auctions of slaves. Buying and selling was done privately. Most new slaves, fresh from Africa, were sold directly from the ships that had brought them across the seas. Michael had often seen men and women and children chained together, naked, scared, being loaded onto the wagons or pettiaugers that would take them to the rice or cotton plantations they'd been sold to. Only once had Michael seen slaves auctioned. A white man had gone bankrupt and his possessions were being sold on the wharf just north of the Exchange, where the customs offices were. A family of seven finely dressed servants stood silently as they were examined and poked and discussed the same as carriage horses in the estate. Michael had stood in the crowd and watched with horror as a pretty little girl was pulled from her mother's arms and sold to a man from Georgia, and the youngest boy was sold to a plantation where the overseer was known to use his lash more often than most. As the family screamed with grief and anger Michael had run from the crowd back to his place on Vanderhorst's Wharf.

Chapter 8

I'm gwine to my heaven,
I'm gwine home, Archangel open the door;
I'm gwine to my heaven, I'm gwine home.
—from "Archangel Open the Door," a South Carolina spiritual

"Michael, come into my office."

Michael looked up in surprise. Captain Linforth didn't talk with his men except when he was giving instructions for the day's work or when someone had done something wrong. What mistake could he have made? Since early morning he and two of the captain's other men had been unloading petti-augers full of cotton from one of the plantations and filling the hold of the lighter with the heavy bales. They were about to sail the *Clarissa* out to the anchored ship in the harbor where a captain was waiting for them to load the crates into his hold.

"Now."

Michael put down his end of a bale and wiped his sweaty forehead. He followed the captain into the office.

"Michael, you're a good worker. I'd be pleased to hire you from Mrs. Lautrec again."

Michael smiled and looked at the captain's feet. He knew the captain's contract with Mrs. Lautrec was almost up, but he hadn't been worried. Like Mama always said: To get along, you go along. "Yes, sir."

"But Mrs. Lautrec died last night."

Michael's head shot up and he looked directly at the captain. "Died?"

"I heard it from someone over on East Bay who's taking word to her son out on Sotherfield. I assume you belong to him now, Michael. If he's willing to hire you out for another year, then I'm willing to sign. But it's too early to know what his plans are."

Michael was silent. Captain Linforth was a fair man. Most people wouldn't have told him about Mrs. Lautrec. He'd have heard it in the streets. Mrs. Lautrec had been kind to Mama and kind to him. He was sorry she had died. She would be in heaven now. She was a strong believer. He wondered if she was with Mama. Were black folks and white in the same heaven?

What would happen to him now? And to Anny and Sam and Sirrah? The spring day that had looked so bright suddenly seemed dark.

"Go on back to loading the cotton, boy. Nothing to be done now. I just wanted you to know."

"Yes, sir. Thank you, sir." Michael went back out of the office onto the wharf. Peter, a free man who worked on the

40

wharf, was weaving a sweet-grass fanner basket the same way his ancestors in Africa had woven fanner baskets for rice fields there. He had interwoven brown and white grasses in regular patterns. *Just like Charleston,* Michael thought. *Brown and white in rows and patterns, tied together by the strength of the palmetto fronds and the sea grasses. Without strong bindings the basket would fall apart. That's what slavery is. The binding that holds all of us together in set patterns.*

Mrs. Lautrec's death meant a break in the pattern of his life. He headed back to the *Clarissa.* Cudjoe and the other men had need of his help with the cotton bales.

All he could do was keep doing what he could do well. What he could do well was be a lighterman.

He tightened his hands into fists. He would have to work and wait while Master Harry and Captain Linforth and the rest of the white folks decided his future.

Chapter 9

Although I here at anchor be
With many of our fleet;
We must set sail one day again,
Our Savior, Christ, to meet.

—inscription on a gravestone, Saint Michael's churchyard, Charleston

"Pay attention, boy!" Cudjoe shouted. But Michael couldn't concentrate. Twice already Cudjoe had corrected his judgment while he was stowing barrels on board a ship out of Liverpool, and once he almost fell off the wharf because he didn't look to see where his feet were taking him.

"You've got to settle down there, now," Cudjoe advised him more quietly. "You don't know what's gonna happen. Could be no changes. You can't do nothin' 'bout it anyways. Just take what's got to be taken." He sounded like Mama.

But Michael didn't want to take any possibility that would send him away from the wharves. And what would happen to Anny and Sirrah and Sam?

Captain Linforth gave him permission to attend Mrs. Lautrec's funeral. Michael pulled on the new white shirt Sirrah had made for him out of the cloth Mrs. Lautrec had given him for Christmas. Sirrah had made the shirt fine and Michael was glad. He wanted to look his best for the funeral.

The bells of Saint Michael's rang, and the nave was filled. Mrs. Lautrec had lived in the city all her life, so there were many people and many kind words said. Her grave was to be dug in the churchyard. She'd be glad to be close to a place she'd loved so much.

Michael sat with Anny and Sam and Sirrah. Master Harry and his wife sat in Mrs. Lautrec's pew, as they did whenever they visited Charleston. Anny cried throughout the service. Some of her tears were for Mrs. Lautrec, Michael knew. But more were out of fear for herself, for her future.

"Mebbe Master Harry be movin' me to Sotherfield where Jim is. Or mebbe he'll be wantin' to keep the big house on Tradd Street for when he and his wife visit the city, and he be needin' a maid there."

Maybe. No one knew.

Michael could hardly sleep at night for the worrying. His dreams were full of Moses and full-sailed ships covered with herons. He woke up drenched with sweat, his heart beating so fast he was sure it would wake the other men.

It was another two days before he heard anything more.

"Michael, come over here. Now, boy!" Captain Linforth called to him while Michael was taking his dinner break with the other men.

He followed the captain immediately.

"Michael, I've talked with Harry Lautrec. He's in need of

43

money, and he's decided to let you stay here and be hired out for another year. Feels you're young and strong, and the more skilled you are, the better."

Michael knew that meant "the more you'll be worth."

"He talked me into increasing the amount I'm paying for your contract, but we agreed on a fair figure. So you'll be working for me into 1807."

Michael grabbed the captain's hand and pumped it up and down. "Thank you, sir, Captain, thank you. I be pleased to work here. Thank you."

The captain pulled his hand away. "Just work as hard as you have been and I'll be pleased too." He turned and went back into his office.

Michael couldn't stop smiling as he returned to the men. "Captain's hired me on for 'nother year. Master Harry agreed. I'm not bein' sold or goin' nowhere."

"Glad to know that," said Cudjoe. "Guess we'll be puttin' up with you for a while more, boy."

Michael worked twice as hard for the rest of the day and grinned at every gull that passed. He wasn't being sold. He wasn't being put in the fields to sweat long hours under an overseer's harsh eyes and whip. He was staying right here on the waterfront in Charleston, where he was valued for his skills as well as his strength. Where he could see the endless horizon and not have his vision blocked by rice or cotton fields. Where he had always wanted to be.

Chapter 10

May be the las' time we eat together
May be the las' time, I don't know.
May be the las' time we drink together
May be the las' time, I don't know.

—from "May Be the Las' Time I Don't Know," a Sea Islands song

That Saturday night Michael allowed himself to be dragged to the Lucky Bag with the rest of the men. They even convinced him to sip some of the watered-down spirits called grog when the proprietor was not watching. People on the docks were used to seeing him with the older men and usually looked the other way. "Boy, you be a sailor, you hav'ta know grog. It's all a sailor's got to drink when he's out to sea and not a thing to say no to," Captain Linforth's other men teased him.

Moses was there too. "This boy," he said, pointing at Michael, "this boy thinks he wants to see snow and ice. Let me tell you about Massachusetts cold. Up north it's so cold some days it would freeze ice between a man and his wife."

The men jostled each other in laughter.

"I wish I could bring some of that New England ice right here and dare Michael to race across it. We'd see how steady on his feet he'd be. He'd really see ice up close then!"

They all laughed, Michael with them, as Moses told them of the special shoes his daughters had—ice skates, he called them—blades like those of knives fastened to leather shoes with straps, which let them glide across the ice. Or tumble down on it, as they often did. "Like chickens in the wind, they fall, squawking, and petticoats flying like feathers." The men couldn't imagine that much ice—most of them had never seen ice at all—and the vision of girls falling with petticoats flying was too much to bear. The grog just made the pictures in their heads funnier, as they then started imagining different animals falling on the ice. On the third round of grog, when someone had just suggested the possibilities of donkeys on skates, Michael felt a heavy hand on his shoulder.

Looking up, he saw Jim.

"Michael, now. We gotta talk." Jim's expression left no question that the talk was important.

Michael nodded and rose, handing some cents to Cudjoe to cover his share of the grog.

Outside, Jim paced up and down the block in the darkness. Men and women, black and white, passed, carrying lanterns, laughing, out for a fine Saturday night. Jim didn't seem to notice. Occasionally a carriage went by, or a man on a horse, and Jim moved out of the way, but that was all.

"What is it?" Michael asked, aware of a tightness inside his own chest. Something was wrong. Very wrong.

After long minutes Jim grabbed Michael's arm and, looking to see that no one was watching, pulled him into a narrow alley.

Jim's fingers were bruising. In the shadows of the taverns and shops, away from the dim light of the moon and candlelight from windows and open doors, Michael couldn't see the expression on Jim's face. "Jim, I's here. I's your friend. I's not goin' away. Let go of me."

Jim loosed his hand suddenly and Michael stepped back, almost hitting his head on the wall of the building. "What is it?"

"Anny." The word was lost in Jim's throat, as though he were choking on it. "Anny. She's gone."

"Gone? Where?"

"Sold. She and Sirrah and Sam. All of 'em. Sold to a slave dealer from the Alabama Territory. Yesterday."

Michael felt the narrow walls of the alley were moving closer to him, locking the two of them between the buildings. Cutting off the air. "You sure? How you know?"

"I left Sotherfield at dusk tonight. Master wasn't there, but the overseer, Mr. Burnside, he gave me a pass to go. Man I knows had a canoe. He brought me. I went to Tradd Street. Ain't no one there; gate's chained shut."

Mrs. Lautrec's beautiful home chained shut? It had never been closed in all the years Michael had lived there. It had always been full of light and people. And the people who lived in the back quarters there had been his family. The only family he'd had after Mama and Papa died.

"I didn't know where to go, what to do. I rattled that gate, wantin' to know. Folks in the street saw me, and I knew the patrol would come and 'rest me for bein' without purpose and disturbin' the peace, but my thinkin' wasn't straight. Then Jemmy, from the Vendreau house? He came out to see 'bout the noise, an' he told me. The rice plantation ain't doin' well; Master Harry be needin' money again. He's sellin' the big house. An' he sold Anny and Sam and Sirrah to a broker yesterday. Just took 'em away and sold 'em!"

"Mebbe they be still in Charleston somewheres." Michael grasped the one hope possible. Trained household slaves were usually sold to other households in the city. Maybe Jim was too worried. Maybe Jemmy had heard wrong.

Jim shook his head. "Jemmy say they sold yesterday 'cause the broker was shippin' out a cargo this mornin'. To Alabama. Heard Mr. Vendreau say so."

Alabama. Slaves sent to the frontier of Alabama were destined for hard work on land being cleared for new cotton plantations. No one ever heard from a brother or mother or sweetheart sold to Alabama.

"Anny's never worked outside of a lady's house. She don't know what it be like, clearin' the land and plantin'."

"She strong, Jim. She be all right." But Michael knew Anny wasn't strong. Chances were she wouldn't be all right. Like Michael, she had been lucky. She had never known a cruel master or the lash or working in the fields from sunup to sundown or sleeping outside before quarters were built. The hardest work she had known was scrubbing fireplace grates and ironing the cotton ruffles on petticoats. Plantation slavery was different from city slavery. Very different.

Jim looked at him. "No way I can get Anny back. I knows that. But I ain't stayin'. Life ain't worth livin' if a man can't protect and care for and love his woman."

Suddenly the silence and shock in Michael turned to anger. It was like losing Mama and Papa again. But this time Master Harry was to blame, not a storm. "No man should be 'lowed to buy and sell people. Split up people that be like families. You an' Anny chose each other. Chose to be together. But Master Harry went and sold her anyway. No man should be able to just up and do that." Michael was glad the darkness hid the tears that came with his anger. He wanted to hit someone or something, or run until his lungs and legs were too sore to feel anything but pain. Anything to take his mind off Anny and Sirrah and Sam being dragged away in chains like those Africans from the ships.

"I thought 'bout you and came lookin'. But you still here. Why didn't he sell you, too?" Jim questioned.

"Captain Linforth's payin' more money to hire me for another year. Master Harry said I'd be worth more then."

Jim shook his fist first toward the street and then toward the sky. There was no place to direct his anger. "So he sells me anytime, and you, he waits till you older and stronger, and then he sells you, too. We have no control over our lives, boy. No say in our futures. I ain't waitin' round for Master Harry to have another bill to pay. And then—who knows what task or master is next? Or after that? A man wants a woman and a family, but I ain't goin' to father any slaves to pay a master's bills."

Michael remembered Papa's words. "You think toward freedom, boy." His mind raced. There were ships in the harbor. Great white angels with sails. Stealing yourself meant danger. Maybe death. But staying—maybe that was another way of dying. Dying in small pieces, one at a time.

Suddenly his thoughts came together. "You goin' to run, Jim?"

"I ain't goin' to stay. Don't make no difference what happens to me no more. I would've run afore, 'cept Anny wouldn't come. And now she be gone. I ain't stayin' no more."

"What you goin' to do?"

"Don' know. Don' know." Jim sank down to the mud and rubble of the alley, his head in his hands. "Don' know."

The door of the Lucky Bag opened to let two young watermen in, and the sound of noisy laughter covered Jim's voice and Michael's thoughts.

Minutes ago he had been one of those laughing inside, sipping grog. Not knowing that Anny and Sirrah and Sam were chained on some vessel—one of those vessels with white angel wings. But that vessel wasn't carrying them to freedom. That vessel was carrying them to an uncivilized wilderness where they would work clearing fields and planting for the rest of their lives.

The grog in his stomach boiled up. Michael gasped, leaned over, and let it all come up, filling his throat and mouth with its bitter stench and spilling out onto the broken oyster shells and sand and mud of the alley.

Chapter 11

Think I heard my captain say
Pay me my money down
T'morrow is my sailin' day
Pay me my money down.

—from "Pay Me My Money Down," a Sea Islands spiritual

*M*ichael stood up. The bitter taste was still in his mouth, but his mind was clear. "Jim, when they be lookin' for you back at Sotherfield?"

"Monday mornin', sunrise."

"No one will be missin' you till then."

"You got an idea?" Jim asked. "You with me?"

Michael nodded. "I be with you. I be thinkin'. But I got to talk with someone first."

"Fewer people knows, fewer people talks."

"But we be needin' help." Michael felt in his pocket. He still had a few cents left from money he'd been paid by a captain whose supplies he'd rowed from Prioleau's Wharf on his own time. He handed the coins to Jim. "You take these an' find someone willin' to sell you a drink." Jim didn't have a letter from Master Harry saying he could buy drink, Michael was certain, but with money in hand he could surely find someone to do the buying for him. "Don't be goin' to the Lucky Bag. Meet me after the curfew bell at Cochran's Wharf. Mebbe by then I'll have a plan. Now I just got an idea. Don't know if it will work."

Jim nodded and looked down at the cents in his hand. "Most folks don't pay no mind to curfew bell Saturday nights 'lessen someone's makin' trouble."

"Hearin' the bell, we can both be there at the same time."

Jim nodded. "Right. Taste of grog would go down real good just now."

Michael could still taste the bitterness in his throat. "Go, then. Give me time. Mebbe I be crazy in the head, like that old man livin' in Stolls Alley and thinkin' he's already in heaven. But there's somethin' I got to try."

Jim turned and walked south on East Bay. After he had gone a few steps, Michael could hear only his footsteps.

Mama had taught him well. All his life he had pushed feelings deep down inside himself so no one knew they were there except probably the Lord. Mama had said it was the only way to survive. Now Michael pushed his anger and fear and misgivings down into his stomach, where they seethed and groaned, but where only he could feel the pain. He hesitated a moment and then went back into the Lucky Bag.

His stomach cramped as smells hit him. He held the cramping with the fear and kept going. The men he'd been sitting with were still there.

"Came back, did you?" Cudjoe asked, moving over to make a spot for Michael on the bench. "Your friend leave?"

Michael nodded. "Just wanted directions. He be gone."

"Some more grog, then!"

"No more grog. My stomach ain't used to it."

"No wonder the boy was gone so long! Well, another time, then. You be young. No reason you should be groggin' now. Time enough for that. Times when you're grown you'll be wantin' it bad. Or not, dependin' on your life."

There was no time to lose. He wanted his life to be whatever he chose it to be. That couldn't happen in Charleston. He had to talk with Moses.

"How long you be stayin' in Charleston, Moses?" Michael asked. "Last time we talkin', you said a week or two."

"Right you are. We'll be casting off and heading out on the tide tomorrow afternoon. Some captains would wait until Monday to sail, but Captain Surridge isn't a churchgoing man. Sundays are just other days to him. We've got a pretty full cargo now, and money can't be made sitting here."

"Passengers?"

"Not that I know of. We're taking fancy goods north. Few ships come to Boston in winter, but they can get into Charleston. We've loaded crates of silk dresses and kid slippers and japanned shawls and lace cloth for the ladies and half a dozen barrels of wigs and a crate of linen drawers for gentlemen. Some shops up on Beacon Hill will be stocked for spring once we get there. One special order too—picked up a dozen crates on King Street yesterday going to someone at Harvard College in Cambridge from his mama."

"So you're full up."

"Just about, I'd say. We checked the ropes and sails and loaded supplies today. Tomorrow we head home."

"How many days' sail be it to Boston?"

"Depends on the winds and the currents and a bit of luck. Given a fair passage, ten days, maybe. Shouldn't be too many storms this time of year. Captain Surridge will probably sail close to shore when he can, keeping away from those English. But the currents that will take us north will keep us offshore, too." Moses rose and stretched. "Got to take a trip to the necessary. Too much grog."

Michael jumped up too. "I be joinin' you."

Cudjoe laughed. "That grog be too much for our boy, I'd say."

Michael laughed with the men, but followed Moses out the back door of the tippling shed. After they'd relieved themselves, Michael touched Moses' arm.

"I needin' your help."

"What is it?" Moses looked at him closely. "Why don't we talk inside, with the others?"

"No. We have to be talkin' private."

Moses walked to a darker corner of the yard. "If you're not wanting Cudjoe to hear something, I'd guess it's something Cudjoe's best not knowing."

"Moses, I got to get out of Charleston. I thought I could live here. Work on the waterfront. Make a life." He took a deep breath. "But a man that's owned can't make a life."

"You just thought of that, boy?"

"I just found out Master Harry sold the folks I grew up with. Close to me, like family, 'specially after Mama and Papa

54

died. All those folks gone. Master Harry be selling me next. Only reason he ain't yet is 'cause I'm bringin' in money, and I'll fetch a bigger price next year or the year after." He looked closely at Moses. "You got a family; you got daughters. One my age. They can plan their futures. Please, Moses. Help me."

Moses took a deep breath and walked a few steps away. What Michael was asking was dangerous. Very dangerous. For both of them. Moses turned back. "What do you want me to do?"

"Hide me tonight on the *Verity*. I be quiet. I won't be needin' nothin' to eat. Mebbe a little water sometimes. That's all. Hide me in the hold of the *Verity*. Take me to Boston."

Michael knew what he was asking. If he was found, not only would he be returned to Charleston in chains, but Moses could also be enslaved. That was South Carolina law.

The silence was a long one.

"I'm not agreeing, Michael. I'm thinking. I might be able to get you on board. Maybe even get you a little water during the trip. But if you're found, you can't say you know me. Can't let Captain Surridge know. You say you sneaked on board yourself. You don't know anything."

"You helpin' me?"

"The crew is on leave and there's darkness to hide you now. My mates wouldn't be ones to look the other way. Ezra Lean and Ben Trader—they'd be the first to turn you in. Captain Surridge don't hold with slavery. I've heard him talk. But if anyone were to know you'd escaped on his vessel, he'd never be able to do business in Charleston again. That's a fact. Harboring fugitives is bad business."

Michael nodded. His clenched hands were still. He could hardly feel his heart beating.

"This your idea? No one else knows?"

Michael hesitated. "There be one other man."

"No!" Moses threw out his arms in anger. "I might help one boy. You look like me when I was young, and Cudjoe says you're a good boy. But two is too risky. It would be a big problem to hide one boy. To hide one man and one boy is too dangerous for all of us."

"He be a carpenter. And young. His sweetheart was sold to the frontier. He's willin' to risk everythin'."

"But am *I* willing to risk everything? And does he know the ways of a vessel on the seas? You know sailing, even if you've never been far to sea. But someone else, not knowing waters?" Moses shook his head and started toward the Lucky Bag's back door. "No; I can't do it."

"Moses, please. Jim's just lost everythin' that be important to him. He my friend, and I's his. I need to help him. He won't be no problem. I promise. You meet him; you'll see."

Moses turned to Michael and sighed. "I don't see. Not at all. But for some reason I'm willing to run the risk of helping you. And maybe your friend. Maybe because I'm free and I see my friend Cudjoe, who is not. I have a wife and three daughters and a house and someday maybe grandbabies. People to love and to take care of me in my old age. Cudjoe has only work. When work is done, what will happen to him?"

Michael didn't answer. There was no answer either of them wanted to hear.

"Maybe this is my time to thank the Lord for being born free." He looked closely at Michael. "If I trust you, you've got to trust me. Don't tell anyone. Don't even tell this Jim who I am. You come back with me and I'll have another drink. I'll look like I've had enough. Then you ask me to take you to see the *Verity*. I'll agree and you help me leave. If I don't agree, then I've changed my mind."

"Thank you." Michael could hardly let the words out.

"I've not done it yet. I haven't figured it. Just let me have that other drink and we'll see."

Chapter 12

I'm goin' to cross that ocean by mysel', by mysel',
I'm goin' to cross that ocean by mysel'.
—from "When My Lord Calls Me I Must Go," a Sea Islands spiritual

The next hour might have lasted a century or an instant; Michael couldn't have told. The men drank and joked. Cudjoe teased Michael about his not drinking, but Michael refused to take even a sip more of the grog. His face was smiling, but his mind was filled with one fear after another.

What if Moses decided not to risk helping him? What if Jim didn't meet him at curfew? What if Jim drank too much tonight and was in no condition to hide? What if they couldn't get water on the *Verity*? What if he couldn't hold still, hidden, for ten days? What if taking this risk would be ending his life?

"Got a long journey tomorrow, friends," Moses finally said, slurring his words and standing up unsteadily.

"You be leavin' us, then?" asked Cudjoe.

"Got to. Got to get back to my wife and daughters. Captain Surridge'll be checking his crew. Got to go back to the brig."

Michael took a deep breath. This was the moment he would know. "Moses, I'd like to be seein' a vessel headin' to that land of ice and snow. Could I go with you to the wharf?"

"Michael, my boy, the *Verity* looks much like any vessel would, headed north or south, but you're welcome to accompany me to her."

Moses was going to help!

Cudjoe leaned over to Michael. "You doin' a kind deed. The grog an' Moses been a mite too friendly tonight. Make sure he be gettin' back to the *Verity* safe."

"I'll see him to the brig. Then I goin' over to Tradd Street to see Sirrah and Anny." Cudjoe knew he sometimes went there on a Saturday night or Sunday, and no one here knew they were gone. No one would miss Michael until Monday morning.

Cudjoe nodded. "Have a good Sunday."

Michael got up and looked at the men. If the future was as he hoped, this would be the last time he would see them. And if his plan didn't work—it would still be the last time. Captain Linforth wouldn't take back a boy who had run. Michael couldn't help it—he reached down and hugged Cudjoe.

The older man looked at him in surprise. "You be takin' care, then, Michael. I be seein' you tomorrow or Monday."

Michael couldn't say anything. He looked again through the smoke and haze at the men he'd worked with for the past year. The men who'd been his family on the waterfront.

"C'mon, boy, if you're comin'," said Moses, heading toward the door. "I got to get back to my brig."

Michael turned and followed. This was his possibility. He had to take it.

As soon as they'd left the Lucky Bag, Moses straightened up and had no problem walking directly up East Bay Street toward Cochran's Wharf. Neither of them spoke.

Suddenly the bells of Saint Michael's rang. It was nine o'clock curfew. After curfew, Charleston law said, all black men and women, slave or free, must be off the streets.

Jim was waiting on Cochran's Wharf in the shadows of a rice warehouse. Seeing Michael, he stepped out, and Michael touched Moses' arm. "My friend Jim. He be here," he whispered.

"He's not to know my name," Moses reminded Michael softly.

Michael nodded and gestured to Jim to join them.

"This be a friend." He indicated Moses. "And this be Jim. Jim, you don't know this man's name nor what he's doin' for us. Don't be rememberin' even his color or his size. He don't exist. But whatever he says, we do."

Jim's breath smelled of rum. He nodded.

"The hold of the *Verity*," Moses said very softly, "is packed with barrels and crates. The safest place would be inside one of those. There are extra barrels behind that cooperage." He pointed to a small shop on the wharf where barrels were made. "Our only chance is now, in the dark. We must get two barrels, one for each of you, and stow them on board. The captain and crew are no doubt dining and drinking in town, so we should be safe if we work quickly. I will give you each a bottle of water and some dried beef. The cook won't notice the little I'll take. You will each get in one of the barrels. I'll put heads on them but not nail them down. That should leave enough space for you to get some air." He looked from Jim to Michael and back again. "I will try to get more food to you, and water, during the journey, but I cannot promise. I will tell no one you are on board. And should either of you be discovered, you must not know me. Say you stowed yourselves on board secretly while we were docked here. Do not reveal each other."

"Thank you, sir. God bless you," said Jim.

"Pray the captain and the tides do likewise," Moses replied. "Let's get those barrels."

It was simple for them to get two empty barrels, and the wooden heads that would top them, to the side of the ship and then lift them in. The packet brig was small. No wonder she could be sailed with a crew of nine. But that meant few places to hide.

The risks were higher than Michael had imagined. He took a deep breath and walked to the railing of the *Verity*. With one movement he pulled his slave badge over his head and threw it as far as he could into the harbor waters. For a moment the brass circle reflected moonlight, and then it sank into the harbor. "Papa, I'm takin' that chance you wanted me to," he whispered to the waters. "I'm gonna be a free man, like you wanted me to be."

Moses gestured at him impatiently. There was no time to hesitate. They climbed down into the hold quickly and secured the barrels that were to be their temporary homes in opposite corners of the hold. "If one of you is discovered, better the other should be as far away as possible. And better you not be tempted to talk with each other, on the chance you'd be overheard."

Michael turned to a larboard corner under the crew's quarters near vessel's bow. It would be the part of the brig most subject to rough waves, and he didn't know how Jim's stomach would manage at sea. Moses and Jim helped Michael get into the barrel. Moses handed in the beef and the Madeira bottle full of water he'd promised, and tapped the barrelhead down loosely.

"Good luck, boy. We'll all be praying."

His legs felt much too long and his elbows were in the wrong places. He sat tightly, knees close to his chest. Almost immediately his calf muscles began to knot. He rubbed them gently. It would be a long ten days. He felt the boat Papa had made for him in his pocket, caught between the barrel side and his leg. It would go with him to freedom. Or wherever else fate would take him.

From the starboard side of the stern he heard the sound of a muffled hammer, which meant Jim was within the other barrel. He was taller than Michael; his body must be even more contorted. Michael heard crates and barrels moving as Moses adjusted the rest of the cargo in front of their hiding places and piled crates where they had been standing.

A harsh voice broke the quiet. "Hey, darky, what you moving barrels and crates for down there? You hiding some monkeys in that hold?"

"Just making sure all is secure, sir," Moses answered.

"There better not be any goods missing when we get to Boston."

"No sir, Mr. Lean."

It was Ezra Lean, the one man Moses had said was most to be feared.

Chapter 13

I'm goin' tuh set in the humble chair
Goin' tuh rock from side tuh side
Goin' tuh rock from side tuh side
Until I die.
—from "Until I Die," a Sea Islands spiritual

Good Lord, help me and help Moses and let Ezra Lean go 'way. Please help us, sweet Jesus. Michael prayed silently. The Lord would hear. After a few minutes Michael heard the cover of the hatch close. Moses must have convinced Lean all was well. Michael's whole body relaxed and he shifted slightly, trying to find a comfortable position.

The rocking of the ship in the shallow water of the harbor at low tide was peaceful. After a time he fell asleep.

Michael wakened suddenly to the choking sound and sour smell that meant Jim's stomach was rebelling against the gentle movement of the waves. He took a small sip of water, knowing his supply might have to last for days. There was nothing he could do for Jim.

He could see nothing. His fingers felt the grain in the wooden barrel. It was hot; warmth from his body had heated the air. The smell of vomit now mixed with the other smells of the vessel: tar, hemp, scrubbed wood, unscrubbed sailors, and the dampness and salt of the waters. The vessel moved and he felt vibrations made by men's feet far above him. The odors were nauseating, and Michael tried to concentrate on the sounds. As hard as he listened, he could hear only muffled sounds that might be voices, far in the distance. Closer, he could hear the scrabbling of rats in the corners of the hold.

He prayed and tried to sleep again. He thought of Mama and Papa. Mama would have told him to stay in Charleston and take whatever would come. Mama hated and feared the seas and the unknown. Papa, he felt sure, would have told him to go. But Mama and Papa were not here. This was his time. He had to make his own decision.

Every minute seemed to take forever. His throat was dry and his stomach groaned, but it was only Sunday morning. They had not even set sail. This was just the beginning. He couldn't eat yet; the beef would have to last. His arms and legs cramped with pain.

Suddenly the boat moved with the waves.

The brig lurched, and Michael was certain. They had cast off. The *Verity* was bound for Boston, with two unanticipated passengers on board.

He and Jim had succeeded; they were leaving Charleston.

He had sailed out of Charleston Harbor many times with Papa, heading to the fishing grounds near the Sea Islands. He didn't need to be on deck now to watch the *Verity* dip and sway as it no doubt followed a small pilot boat around the long wharves, past the Exchange and grand houses of South Bay Street, between the anchored vessels, and through the Middle Channel. As they passed Sullivans Island the steeple of Saint Michael's would be the last Charleston landmark to stay in view.

Soon he would meet new people, make new decisions, live a new life. A free life. "Pleased to be meetin' you. My name is Michael Lautrec," he imagined himself saying, per-haps to a captain who would hire him or a man who would befriend him or even someday to a pretty girl.

Michael Lautrec. Mama had named him for the church she loved. "Your name is for Saint Michael. Saint Michael be a powerful strong angel. He fought with the wicked and he won. You be strong too." How many times had Mama told him that?

He never heard his name without thinking of the church. And of Mama.

The only last name he'd ever had was that of the Lautrec family. The name given to him because he was owned.

"NO!" Michael shouted the word out without realizing it. He froze. Had anyone heard him?

But no one came. Jim must have heard him but hadn't replied. And no one above had heard him over the shipboard sounds of ropes and waves and the creaking hull.

He was safe.

"No." He said it again, softly. "Michael Lautrec was a

slave boy. I be a free man now, makin' my future." He was sure. Michael Lautrec, the obedient Charleston slave, was gone. But who was he now? Whoever he was, he needed a new name. A name defined a person.

What would his name be?

He could take an African name. Mama's Gambian name was Affiba, meaning she had been born on a Friday. But no—he was this-country born and making his life on this side of the waters. And Papa had only a slave name, like Michael. He had been called Big Billy, for his height. He had not been given a last name. Michael wanted two names. Names that a person could hear and know something about him besides. The names must be right. He needed powerful names to strengthen him, like Saint Michael's had.

The hull groaned as the brig resisted the waves; he could feel the vibrations of the wind on the shrouds and sheets far above him. He imagined the vessel as he had always dreamed it would look: like an angel, its white wings carrying him far from the city.

He wanted a name that showed his love for the sea. His love for the church. His pride in who he was. A name that did not apologize for who he was born to be.

He thought of all the names he had heard. A Bible name would be best. There was Adam, Abraham, Joshua, Moses. He smiled, thinking of his friend on the decks above. That was a right name. A new name would be safer, too; anyone searching for Michael Lautrec from Charleston would never find someone who went by the name of . . . Noah Brown.

That was him. He knew it the moment the name appeared in his mind. Noah was the captain God trusted most. And although Michael was African and therefore "black," his own skin color was lighter than that of many Africans. Papa's white father had ensured that. African blood must be mighty, since even one drop of black blood was more important to most folks than ten drops of white blood. He was African American, for sure. But his color was brown.

Michael smiled. No one ever questioned a man's name. Only he would know Noah Brown's name meant both who he had come from and who he was going to be.

"Noah Brown." He whispered it over and over to himself. The more he said it, the more he liked it. "Noah Brown."

Chapter *14*

I am huntin' for a city, to stay awhile,
I am huntin' for a city, to stay awhile;
I am huntin' for a city, to stay awhile,
  O, believer, got a home at las'.
—from "Hunting for a City," a South Carolina spiritual

*N*oah dozed off and on. The rolling of the ship swayed him gently from side to side, like a mother rocking him in a cradle. The ship moaned as the boards of the hull met the currents of the sea. As Noah dozed his dreams were of Mama.

The straining boards surrounding him turned, in his mind, to the moans of Africans, tied, imprisoned, unknowing, and afraid. Mama had told him about her journey to Charleston. She had been only a girl, eight years old, when she was captured with a woman from her village while they walked together to the rice fields. Tied and silenced, frightened by the black countrymen who had captured and imprisoned her, she was forced to lie in a canoe for two days' journey. And then, when the canoe stopped, hardly able to walk, she was half pushed and half carried to a large stone building, where her captors now had white faces. Mama's voice would laugh as she told the story of the little girl—tied and tired and hungry, crying for her mother—who thought white folks were ghosts. But her eyes never laughed.

"We was so scared. Lord, we was scared. We was thinkin' those white folks was goin' to eat us. Nobody ever seen black folks come back from white folks' ships. And we was sailin' west, toward where my people knew heaven be.

"We was all chained, both arms and legs, even the children. On some ships, I've heard folks say, they let children run free, and even some women. Those women weren't free; just not in chains. But the ship I was on, the *Eagle*, held so many women and children—over a hundred of us—that we was all chained. Men chained in one place; women and children in another. The woman I was chained to was round with child. She had that baby right there, in her chains, on the ship. No water to clean her or soothe her. No hands to reach and help, though we was all hearin' her screams. That baby never cried. It was born dead. I never knew if it be a boy or a girl. I wanted terribly to know. Just know if it be a boy or girl. But a white man came and threw its body overboard before I could see. The next day its mama died, and the men came and unchained her from me and threw her overboard too. So mama and baby stayed together."

As the *Verity* moved slowly northward Noah thought of that little girl who had been his mother, chained to a dead woman, lying in the blood and vomit and piss and excrement of dozens of frightened people. The barrel that held him was dry and clean and secure. He still had most of his bottle of water left and some pieces of beef. If Mama endured, he could endure.

It could have been day or night. The ship rocked and groaned, and the sounds of the sea rolled together. Sometimes one of the rats in the hold would scratch the outside of his barrel. They smelled the little bits of beef he had hidden under his shirt, close to his body. Once in a while he would nibble a piece so small he could hardly taste it. If he allowed himself to really taste it, and the salt on it, he would want it too much and be too tempted to eat. The food had to last.

Mama had had only gruel to eat on her voyage, and a little water that cramped her stomach. The smells in the hold were bad, and if the food didn't nauseate you, then the stench would. The children and women tried to talk with one another, but they came from different parts of Africa, and only a few recognized words from other languages. They were locked in the hold of the monster ship, being taken for some unknown purpose to some unknown place, and locked inside their own minds, since words no longer functioned. All they shared was hunger and pain and muscle spasms and their own bodies' filth and shame and fear.

"Not bein' able to talk with someone. Tell someone your name and where your village was and what you feared. That was the worst of all. Not knowin', and bein' alone, even though there was hundreds of us on that ship. We was alone, and yet if we moved even a little, to wiggle our toes or stretch our arms in their sockets, we touched other flesh." Mama's eyes would fill and her hands would shake as she remembered her journey.

71

Noah, too, was alone. His body touched only the sides of the barrel. The muscles of his fingertips and knees and back memorized the grain of every board. He knew where every nail was and how far each one stuck out.

When heavy swells lifted the *Verity* and dropped her suddenly, those nails cut into him. He felt the drops of blood slowly dripping down his skin and then hardening. He was like one of the small stones tinsmiths placed inside a rattle for a baby to play with. He never knew when the rattle would be picked up, flinging him from one side of the barrel to the other.

How had Mama survived? This journey might take ten days. He kept his thoughts focused, to stay alive, not to scream with the muscle pain and the loneliness and the fear. Mama's journey had taken four weeks, as close as she could guess.

"I thought I'd never be breathin' clean air again, or have clean skin, or have enough to eat or drink. I thought this was the way white ghost people lived, floatin' on the waters forever." Mama would shake her head. "Carolina land looked like heaven when that ship finally stopped. I didn't care what happened to me then. Nothin' could've been worse than bein' in that ship's hold. I could hardly walk for stiffness and pain when those other white men came to drag us away. But all I cared 'bout was seein' the sun and feelin' it on my body. I could hardly feel the chains anymore or the whips."

"And that's how you came home, Mama," Noah would say when he was little.

And Mama would reply, "That's how I came to this place that is my home for now, and home to you, my darlin' boy. My real home be lyin' 'cross those waters. When I die, I be goin' home an' joinin' my mother and my father and the mothers and fathers of my mother and father. But the moon followed me here to this America, and it will follow you wherever your life leads. You will see the moon and you will never be alone."

Noah hoped Mama was with her family in Africa now and that the Jesus she had found at Saint Michael's Church was right there with them. He'd made sure she was buried with her head to the west, toward the hereafter, and had secretly taken a cup and plate from the mistress's kitchen and shattered them on Mama's grave to break the chain of death so no one else in the household would die. He had put shells on her grave—luminous mermaid's toenails and white angel wings and brown-banded tulip shells—as Mama had done for other Africans who had died.

He wished he could look up now and see the moon and not feel so alone.

There was no one to see his tears, so he cried for Mama and for Papa and for Anny and Sirrah and Sam. He cried for himself, for all his fears. He cried until he slept, and dreamed of being chained in lines on a ship. He dreamed of being tied onto the back of an eagle, high in the sky, following the North Star. He dreamed of casks of water and of rain falling from the sky onto his body and into his mouth.

After a while he didn't know how long he dreamed, or which thoughts were real and which imagined. He didn't know when he was awake and when he slept.

All he knew were the walls of the barrel, holding him, protecting him, imprisoning him. On his way to freedom.

Chapter 15

Yes, soon as the packet is well out to sea,
'Tis cruel, hard treatment o' every degree.

—verse of a sea chantey, sung to the tune of "Blow the Man Down"

There was no way to know how much longer it had been, or how much farther they had sailed, when he heard the gunshots.

At first, waking out of a dream, Noah thought they had hit a sandbar or a rock. But the brig continued to move, pitching heavily. Then she turned slightly, although it might have been the natural turning of a ship in heavy seas.

The noise came again. Like thunderclaps, it had a vibration to it. It was nearby. Then there were more explosions even closer. He had never heard the sounds before, but he knew immediately what they were. Another vessel was firing at the *Verity.*

He concentrated on not panicking. He listened. He heard no rushing water, which meant that, so far, the hull had not been hit. The *Verity* was a small packet brig, not likely to carry guns herself. And a schooner or larger brig or, even more likely, a man-of-war—the sort of vessel to carry guns—could outrun her easily.

But why? Why would another vessel of any size have cause to fire on them?

The *Verity* was laden with goods; the vessel giving them chase might be a pirate ship or privateer. But piracy was a danger of the past, talked of only in tavern tales. Privateers, ships of war commissioned to take other ships as prizes, were common enough during wartime. But the United States was not at war. The *Verity* swayed and her planks moaned. Captain Surridge was pushing her to make some distance. If another vessel was pursuing, they must be too far from land to seek help.

Noah heard a muffled sob from the far corner of the hold. Jim, too, knew their danger.

Then—silence. The guns had stopped. The *Verity* was slowing.

Whoever was in pursuit had won.

As the rhythm of the waves hitting the side of the *Verity* slowed, Noah's heart beat faster.

What would this mean for him and for Jim? If the ship was boarded for her cargo, then he would be carried with the hats and wigs and other fine goods onto some other ship, headed in some other direction. If he climbed out of the barrel, he would be discovered, put in chains, and returned to Charleston, or be put in custody and confined at the vessel's destination.

What if he was wrong and there were still pirates? What if seamen seized the *Verity* and took what goods they wanted and then killed the crew? Moses was probably on deck watching the approaching vessel at this moment. What if they burned the *Verity*? Or shot her full of holes to sink her and conceal whatever they were about to do?

Escaping Charleston had been a terrible mistake. He could be back on Vanderhorst's Wharf right now, working with Cudjoe and feeling the spring sunshine on his back and face. He could have something in his stomach other than hunger cramps. He had taken a chance, he had gambled, and he had lost. This was the end.

He could see nothing inside of the dark barrel. But suddenly he heard the hatch opening. Men were climbing down the ladder. Had he and Jim been discovered already? Noah almost stopped breathing for fear. Two more men were now in the hold.

"They'll find us down here for sure. The place stinks worse than usual, too."

"Not for sure," answered another, deeper voice. "Could be they're just in need of one or two men and they'll find them on the deck or in quarters. Above the hold. Hold your nose."

"My father fought those Brits in the war. I ain't doin' their fighting for them now!" That voice was a boy's.

Now Noah knew what was happening! The *Verity* was being boarded by a British navy man-of-war seeking to impress sailors. These other men were going to do what Jim and Noah had already done: hide among the barrels and crates in the hold.

"Over there—there's space enough aft to hide between the line where twelve barrels front on eleven. I'm going forward, behind those crates."

"I just want to go home to Providence." It was the boy.

"Wouldn't we all like to be home. I'd like to be with my wife or be sitting in a tavern with a tankard of ale before me. But that ain't today, boy." The man stumbled. "This place is darker than a cave at midnight." His voice softened. "Just find a corner, get down in it, and be quiet. You'll be home with your ma soon enough."

Noah heard them moving crates and barrels. One of them was coming closer and closer to his hiding place. Someone shifted his barrel. The man was hiding next to him, only inches away. He could smell the tar and sweat on the man's body. He hoped the man couldn't smell him. There had been no place to relieve himself other than where he hid.

Was Moses hiding too?

In a far corner of the hold he heard a rat squeak. Maybe the boy had disturbed another small hiding place.

There was a dull thud and the *Verity* shuddered.

"Must be their longboat. They're comin' on board." The whisper of the man next to him thundered in Noah's ear.

Chapter 16

Believer, O shall I die?
O my army, shall I die?
Jesus die, shall I die?
Die on the cross, shall I die?

—from "Shall I Die," a South Carolina spiritual

*I*t seemed forever before the hatch opened again.

Many footsteps descended this time.

"Listen up," said a very loud and very English voice. "We know this brig wasn't sailing with a crew of seven, which is the number of men we found above. We know you're down here. 'Twill be easier for all of us if you just stand up and show yourselves."

Noah held his breath. No one moved.

"Then, we'll have to search you out and it won't be as pleasant for anyone." Another moment of silence. "Marshall, there are no gentlemen of honor here. You start aft; I'll go forward. Patterson, stand guard and watch for any movement."

"Yes, sir."

There were at least three of them, then.

Crates were being pushed and barrels shoved. "Just stick your sword into corners. That'll get 'em out soon enough." It was the first voice again.

Noah heard three crates being picked up and dropped. Those must have been the light ones; perhaps they held the wigs or some other fancy goods. Sounds were getting closer. A sailor's sword hit the hull of the ship rhythmically, checking between the barrels.

Suddenly his barrel moved and he heard a scream, very close. He bit his lip hard to keep from making a noise. He tasted blood as his lip swelled.

"Found one of 'em!"

The man hiding within inches of Noah stood up. "You got my arm. How you expect me to be of use to anyone with a bleedin' arm?" The man tripped as he was pulled from his hiding place.

"If you hadn't been cowering down there like a cornered rat, you'd have had no injury. Afraid to stand up and be counted like men, these former colonists are. British navy'll teach 'em a thing or two about being real sailors."

"I've no interest in being part of your stinking navy," spit out the American. "If I'd wanted that, I'd have sailed out of Bristol, England, not Bristol, Connecticut."

"Just shut up and stay still. Patterson, hold him. You didn't hide down here alone."

Noah waited. The English sailor who had been near his barrel had apparently decided no one else was there; he hadn't returned. Noah wondered how bad the man's arm was and held his own wrist tightly. A sword cut could go to the bone.

Another crash and a call. "It's me! Don't use your sword. I'm coming out."

The boy.

"Come on, then, and make it quick. Looks like we got your shipmate there. Another rat hiding in the corner."

Crash!

"Praise the Lord, there's a third one over here. A stinking black one in a barrel. Out of there, you. Now!"

They'd found Jim. What would they do? Would Jim say anything about him?

"I'm thinking this one is a bonus. Looks like a surprise to these other boys here, am I right? Well, get him over here with the other two, and let's take them on deck."

"Please, please, master. I ain't no sailor. Let me be!" Jim's voice was a cry. Then there were no more voices, only the sound of stumbling feet that no doubt belonged to Jim, since he had been as cramped as Noah was still.

"Up with all of you stinking lot. Onto the deck!"

"Please, sir. Please!"

Noah heard the squeaking of heavy feet on the ladder and then the hatch slammed shut.

He was alone.

Chapter 17

Noah heard stomping and raised voices from above, but nothing clear enough to tell him what was happening on deck.

At any moment they could come back down and find him. At any moment the *Verity* could be sunk. At any moment anything could happen.

Would the British ship take the crew and leave the *Verity* adrift? Or take her as plunder, as privateers would? There were valuable goods in the hold. *He* was in the hold.

Noah counted his heartbeats, trying to keep his mind calm. He had reached 948 when he heard the hatch open and footsteps climb down the ladder.

"Michael, boy, are you all right?" Moses' voice was low and kind.

Noah broke into quiet tears of relief. "I be fine," he said, his voice shaking. "What happened?"

"The British boarded us. They impressed three of the crew and your friend Jim."

"No—not Jim!"

"He told them he was no sailor, but a carpenter. Turned out they had need of a carpenter—their man was washed over in a gale weeks past, and repairs were needed. So they took Jim. Said they'd teach him to be a sailor."

"He just wanted to be free!"

"Well, that he'll be. There are no slaves in the British navy, and they won't be returning him to his master in Charleston, that's for certain."

So Jim would have a life, free, in the British navy. He was young and strong. Maybe he'd do all right.

"Michael, are you listening?"

"Yes. But I be Noah Brown now. A new name for a new life." It seemed strange to be saying his chosen name out loud.

"A fine name. Well, then, Noah Brown, here's the situation. They took three of us. Jack, the cook, because they were in need of a cook as well as a carpenter. And two of the younger men. I was lucky—they judged me too old to be of use."

"Did they take Ezra Lean?"

"No, more's the pity. He and Ben Trader are still with us. But the captain was sailing with a tight crew before. Now he has only six men left. And one is still a boy and one injured."

They must have left the man they had cut, who had hidden near Noah, and the boy with him.

"The captain is talking of returning to Charleston to find more mariners."

"No!" Not back to Charleston! Noah would be found for sure and taken to Captain Linforth or Master Harry. He would be lashed until he couldn't move and then sold. Or killed.

"I have an idea. But the idea is full of risk, so think it through. You can sail—you know ships, even if most of your sailing has been in protected harbors. With seven men and the captain we might be able to continue. If I tell Captain Surridge you are here, would you be willing to work for your passage?"

"But if folks knew the captain helped me, he'd lose Carolina trade." Noah remembered Moses telling him of the captain's love of the delights of the city.

"True enough. But the captain wants to get back to Boston; he wants to get far from the British, deliver his cargo, and go home to his wife. I don't know for sure he will agree. He could put you in chains and return to Charleston to claim the reward that no doubt has been posted. But it might be worth a try."

Noah's thoughts raced. "If I don't show myself, then most likely we'll return to Charleston and I'll be discovered in port."

"But the choice is yours." Moses hesitated. "Since I know you're on board, I am also liable. You know the laws about helping a slave escape."

Moses was suggesting a major risk for himself when he said he would talk to Captain Surridge. Greater in many ways than Noah's risk. Noah was already a slave.

The walls of the barrel suddenly seemed safe and comforting.

"Talk to your captain. I be willin' to help if he be willin' to have me."

"I'll go now, then. The captain is already plotting his course back to Carolina." Moses paused. "If he accepts you, freedom will be worth the gamble."

"And if he not be willin'?"

"Then I'll join you on an auction block in Charleston, where you'll end your life as Michael." Moses' footsteps retreated.

Chapter 18

*W*ithin minutes Noah heard the hatch open again. This time there was also the sound of many voices.

"So you did hide a monkey down here, did you?" Noah recognized Ezra Lean's voice and then heard several men laughing.

Then another voice. "I ain't sailin' with no slave."

"Take it easy. I'm captain and I decide who sails with whom. Smith may have found a way to help us get home. That's what we all want now. Although I don't look forward to talking to the wives of those three lost men."

"Yes sir, Captain."

The footsteps came closer to Noah, and then the barrels nearest to him were moved.

"Here he is, sir." Moses' voice.

"Well, then, let's see him."

Noah felt pressure on the side of the barrel. It moved slightly as the barrel head was opened.

"Stand up, Michael . . . Noah."

Moses offered him a strong hand.

Noah straightened his back and legs as he tried to stand. His right leg was so cramped it would bear no weight for a moment. Moses tipped the barrel slightly and then reached and helped him climb out.

There were seven other men in the hold. Noah immediately picked out the boy who had hidden. He was much younger than the rest, slim and freckled, his nose reddened by the sun. One of the men was, like Moses, older than the rest. One of the other five men had a crude white bandage around his forearm. One had a wide, whitened scar across his left cheek, just as Moses had described it in the tippling shed. Ezra Lean.

"Boy, come over here." The tall man in the center seemed to be the captain.

Noah stumbled forward, still uncertain of his footing.

"The stinkin' monkey can't even walk! How can he sail?" Lean said.

Captain Surridge ignored his comment. "Smith tells me you know ropes and winds."

"Yes, sir."

"Where have you sailed?"

"In Charleston Harbor, sir. And in smaller boats, been sailin' out to the Sea Islands for fish."

"Well, we won't be doing much fishing on board the *Verity*." The Captain looked him up and down. "What's your name and your age?"

Noah stood straight. "Noah Brown, sir. I be fourteen."

The captain walked around him, staring the way a buyer would. "You're big for your age, Noah Brown. I would have guessed you at least sixteen. You look considerably older than Johnny, here, who is thirteen." He gestured at the other boy. "You and your friend hiding here put me at great risk."

"Yes, sir."

"Why did you do it?"

"To get to freedom, sir. To get to a place where I could make my own future."

The captain stared at Noah for a long moment before speaking. "Well, you'll be making your future here for right now. I have no desire to return to Charleston, and neither do any of the men here. But you and every other man on this brig will have to work with little break for the next week if we're to get to Boston. We'll work four hours on, four hours off, and all hands on deck whenever we shorten sail or tack." Captain Surridge paused. "And there'll be no regular meals, as our cook is gone."

Noah spoke up. "Sir, I can cook some. My mama be a cook. She taught me."

The captain looked at him. "Well then, boy, you just volunteered for another job. Blacks make good cooks. Smith, you take him up and show him where supplies are stored. We'll see if he can pull together a meal. The rest of you—topside! Head northeast. We're sailing home."

Moses steadied Noah's balance as they climbed the ladder out of the hold. He said quietly, "So far so good. Just stay clear of Ezra Lean and Ben Trader."

Noah remembered Papa saying, "Never hurts none to know how to get things done." Who would have thought he'd be sailing—and cooking—on a deepwater brig?

But Papa had also said, "You got to know which folks to trust and which not." Could he trust Captain Surridge?

Chapter *19*

The work wuz hard, an' the voyage wuz long,
The sea wuz high an' the gales wuz strong.

—from "Leave Her, Johnny, Leave Her," a sea chantey

*W*orking on that brig wasn't easy.

The vessel wasn't big enough to have a galley; cooking was done in a one-man-size box called the caboose, which was lashed to the deck and contained a stove. There Noah combined rice, wheat flour, water, and salt to make flat johnnycakes for the crew to go with the salted pork he soaked and boiled. It was far from Mama's shrimp pie and tomato red rice, but there were no complaints. No one else on board knew enough to have given them that. And, most important to tired and hungry seamen, there was plenty and grog to wash it down.

The grog on board was more watered than that in port,

and Noah's stomach managed it. He wished for vegetables, for seasoning as well as for texture and taste, but the previous cook hadn't provided any. Cooks in Charleston made daily trips to the vegetable and fruit vendors near the wharves. Cooking at sea was not like cooking in Charleston.

But cooking was the easy part of the journey.

"Hey, boy." Ezra Lean's face always seemed too close at hand. "Boy, you been out in the sun too many years? You and Moses make a pair. Without a lantern you'd both look like shadows in the dark, if it weren't for those teeth of yours!" Lean seemed to find that thought greatly amusing, as he repeated it regularly.

"Boy, you may think Capt'n Surridge is doing you a favor, letting you work for him. But when we get to Boston, he'll turn you over to the nearest slave catchers 'fore you know where Faneuil Hall is. There's money to be made from returning runaways to their rightful places. And if the capt'n doesn't make the time to do so, then Ezra Lean will take care of that himself. You can be sure of that." Lean leered at him, whispering threats and possibilities whenever Noah was near.

"Don't let him trouble you," Moses counseled. "When we dock in Boston, we'll go ashore together. I have friends. You'll come and stay with me."

Although they all worked closely together and slept on narrow berths in the same space, the other mariners tried to keep a distance from Moses and Noah. They were quiet, but sometimes it was clear they agreed with Lean. Lean was not still, and to Noah he seemed to be everywhere. And where he wasn't, Ben Trader was.

"You blacks should go back to Africa, where you belong. I

seen pictures of Africa. People there ain't civilized. Monkeys, running round naked. You feel uncomfortable in clothes, you go right ahead and take 'em off. Or maybe you'd like a little help." Trader swiped his knife clean through Moses' shirt. "Black folks need to know their place. Stay down in those cotton fields with their own kind. Not thinking they're good as white." He looked directly at both Moses and Noah. "Not taking work away from white men."

Noah watched as Moses ignored his comments and moved away from Trader. Noah wanted to defend them both—tell Trader they were men, same as white men—but he followed Moses' lead and swallowed his responses. Moses was a free man. If he didn't respond to the taunting, Noah mustn't.

Even when an African man was free, Noah saw, he was not treated as other men. In Charleston, Noah had learned well to hold emotions in and not to show feelings. Here, where he and Moses were the only blacks on the brig, he was afraid. Just as Ezra Lean meant him to be. White men had the power.

Making port in Boston no longer meant freedom. It might mean the shackles of slave catchers. And every day they were closer to Boston.

But there was little time to think of the future. The bowsprit pointed to the northern horizon, and there was wind enough to fill the sails. Sailing in Charleston Harbor had not prepared Noah's muscles for the strain of sheeting topsails in a strong sea breeze, but every day he was thankful for all he had learned from Cudjoe and Captain Linforth. They had been good teachers, and he could hand, reef, steer, and climb the rigging with the best of them. Captain Surridge occasionally corrected him, but as often nodded approval.

"Captain Surridge's pleased with your work. Told me this would be a trip to remember, but it looked as though we'd make it all of a piece and we couldn't have come through it without your help." Moses smiled at him. "You're doing fine, Noah." Noah hoped Jim was doing fine too. He wondered what vessel Jim had found himself on and what he was doing. What was it like for a plantation slave to become a British sailor?

Noah kept his thoughts to himself and barely spoke with the other men. He didn't know them, and not knowing meant not trusting. He watched them and he measured their worth. Moses was right. They were all, except for the boy, Johnny, expert mariners who worked hard and slept hard and had little to say in between. Johnny might have been close to Noah's age, but he was much younger in spirit. Once or twice he tried to talk with Noah. But Noah couldn't bring himself to trust a white boy from the North. And Johnny's questions were endless.

"What was it like to be a slave, Noah?"

"It be just a way to be born and to live." Noah was standing near the caboose and could see the whole run of the deck. Supper was done, it was a fair day, and the men seemed relaxed. The captain had told them two more days' good sailing should take them into Boston Harbor.

"Were you ever lashed?" Johnny leaned in eagerly.

"No." Noah thought of the long, raised welts on Mama's back.

"Did they chain you and starve you?"

Noah looked at this well-fed young boy. Perhaps in Johnny's mind being deprived of sweets might constitute starvation. The boy often hung around the caboose, asking Noah if he had any sugar.

"Be no cause to chain me or starve me. And how could I be 'spected to work if I was chained or starved?"

"Where are your mother and father?"

"Dead. They both be dead." Noah turned to him. "Your mother and father?"

"I'm sorry about your parents. My father is a merchant in Providence. That's in Rhode Island. He wanted me to learn about the sea because the goods he sells come by ship, from Europe mostly. And I was tired of school. My mother takes care of our house and my brothers and sisters. Do you have brothers and sisters?"

"No," Noah answered. He wondered how many servants Johnny's mother had to help her run the house and care for the children. "You didn't want no more schoolin'?"

Johnny shrugged. "It was boring. I can read and write and cipher. What more do I need to know?"

Noah could not imagine what there was to know. He could not even imagine knowing how to read and write and cipher.

"When we get to Boston, you'll be free, won't you? No one is a slave in Boston."

"So folks say," Noah replied, tightening a rope that had loosened.

"I've heard the men talking. They say if you're returned to your master, then the one who returns you will get a big reward."

"Do they?" Noah grasped the cap rail tightly.

"If someone tried to return you to Charleston, what would you do?"

I would fight them. I might even kill them, Noah thought. *I will not go back.* He said, "Charleston is a far way from Boston."

Johnny shrugged and moved on.

The breeze was turning northerly, freshening somewhat. There was clear, open water ahead. When would they see land? They were but a few miles from the coastline and would have to tack back and forth to go against the wind. Any minute the captain would call for all hands.

The air was fresh and the early May sun warm. The farther north they sailed, the darker blue the waters were. Day breezes were cooler and night winds were cold. The blocks creaked and the wind hummed in the taut sails. The sea foam hissed and swished alongside. One of the men sang a song of the sea and of the voyage home.

Home. Where was home now? What would life away from Charleston be like? Noah pushed those thoughts to the back of his mind. First he had to get to Boston. Once he had found a place, then he could think of finding ways to stay there.

He stood like all seamen, his feet apart, planted heavily on the deck to keep his balance on the rolling vessel. His bare feet were heavily callused, but they still felt the sting of the ropes. The other mariners wore leather shoes or low boots, but he had none. He looked up at the sails and rigging. He had climbed to the top of that rigging and done his share of setting the canvas. From here the sails did not look like angels' wings. They were filled by the wind, and the feel of their weight and strength was now too familiar to his hands and arms and back for him to think of them as heavenly. They were man made, set by men to catch the breezes of the heavens and to help direct them to shore.

"Hey, boy . . . dreaming of Charleston?" It was Ezra Lean. "Don't you worry none. You'll be back there sooner than you know. Two more days till we arrive in beautiful Boston Harbor. Wonder if the captain—or maybe your old friend Ezra—will let you walk on a Boston wharf or street before finding a ship headed back to that fine city in South Carolina that you miss so much. There'd be many a captain glad to deliver merchandise south. Especially when he knew there was payment due at the delivery port."

Noah held himself tight and pretended not to hear. He remembered one of Mama's sayings: "Talking 'bout fire doesn't boil the pot." Ezra Lean was only talking.

Lean moved closer, speaking directly into Noah's ear. "You just breathe deep, slave boy. Because in two days you'll be breathing your last free air. Slaves stay with their masters; that's the way it is. Law says so. Can't have some black boy who thinks he's as good as a white man changing the way the world is, can we?"

It took all of Noah's strength not to speak and not to turn. If he said anything, if he did anything, that would give Ezra Lean a reason to fight him. And fighting would give Captain Surridge a good reason to turn him over to the slave catchers in Boston.

But Noah was afraid. Afraid that what Ezra Lean said was true. Afraid his own anger and fear would erupt, leaving his thoughts and feelings open so other people could see them.

Letting other folks see inside of him would be worse than chains. There were many ways one man might own another, but no one would ever own his thoughts.

"Time I be startin' supper," Noah said calmly. "Eight men on board be wantin' food soon enough."

"Seven men'll be eating, boy. You forgot—you're not a man. You're only a slave," taunted Ezra Lean. But he turned and moved toward the stern as Noah unclenched his fist and headed to the hold to get the dried apples he had found there earlier. He could stew them with a little sugar, and even Johnny would be pleased.

Only two more days. He had to hold his temper for two more days.

Chapter 20

Oh, shinin' is the North Star,
As it hangs on our stabbud bow.
We're homeward bound for Boston Town,
An' our hearts are in it now.

—from "The Sailor's Way," a nineteenth-century sea chantey

*W*inds had taken them around Nantucket Island and Cape Cod, and Captain Surridge had no need of a pilot to show him how to navigate the channels of Massachusetts Bay. Boston Harbor was in sight.

"Ezra Lean says he'll turn me over to the slave catchers!" Noah whispered to Moses. "How can I run in a city I don't know?"

"Don't leave the *Verity* without me," Moses counseled. "Where I live you won't stand out to those looking."

Noah nodded. Moses had already risked his own freedom to help Noah gain his; he did not want Moses to have to risk more. But he knew no one else. For now he would have to depend on Moses.

"Will I have to hide? Will Lean and Trader follow us?" Noah whispered again when he and Moses were alone near the caboose.

Moses was not as reassuring as Noah had wished. "In Boston you must stay out of sight for a while. They will lose interest and be shipping out again. For now, just think of getting off the *Verity* and through the streets of Boston. After they lose sight of you—as we'll make sure they do—Lean and Trader and their friends will no doubt spend their first night in port at a tavern. That will give us time."

If only Moses were right!

In all his thinking about stealing himself and hiding on board, never once had Noah thought of debarking as a challenge. Thank goodness he had someone to help him.

As a series of long wharves came into view and Noah finished cleaning the caboose, Captain Surridge came and spoke to him. "Noah, you've seen us through, and I have no desire for you to be sent south, as some would have it."

Noah waited.

"I assume you have planned to leave the ship with Moses?"

"Yes, sir."

"Both of you wait until I disembark."

"Yes, sir!"

Captain Surridge would also help him arrive safely! Even Ezra Lean listened to Captain Surridge.

After they were tied fast to the dock, the captain called his crew together. "Men, it is late in the day, and I know you are anxious to see your families or pursue other entertainments."

There were a few nudges and whispered comments from the men.

"It has been a more difficult trip than any of us imagined. I must now go to the homes of the three men we lost and speak with their wives and mothers. It is not a task I take lightly. You are now free to leave the *Verity*. But we have a cargo to unload and accounting to be done. I expect all of you back here at daybreak. No wages will be paid until the *Verity* is unloaded and in condition to sail again." He looked at them all. "Any questions?"

There were none.

"Moses Smith and Noah Brown will go with me tonight to represent the crew in expressing their condolences." He turned to Moses. "You know the home of Jack Strong?"

Moses nodded. Strong was the black cook who had been impressed.

"That is where we will go first. I'll see the rest of you men at dawn. Be sharp!"

The five other men clamored onto the dock and headed in various directions. Ezra Lean looked back several times and cursed. "Slave lover!" he hissed.

"The captain's going to keep the reward money for himself. You'll see!" added Trader.

Captain Surridge ignored them. "Am I right in assuming Jack Strong's home is near yours?"

"Yes, sir. Not far from it," Moses replied.

"We will go there quickly, since I have to bear sad tidings to three families and would like to see my own wife before the sun has set too far."

Noah followed Moses through the narrow streets, with

Captain Surridge behind him. Dogwood and cherry trees, which had stopped blooming two months ago in South Carolina, were just budding here. Brick buildings were dark red, not brown, as they were in Charleston. Streets were covered with pebbles and stones instead of oyster shells.

Moses finally stopped in front of a small whitewashed house. "This is Jack Strong's home."

The captain hesitated. "Moses, take Noah and go wherever you feel best. I expect to see you back at the dock tomorrow morning. But Noah, I don't expect to see you."

Noah opened his mouth to say that he could come, and then realized the captain was ensuring his distance from Ezra Lean and the others. "Thank you, Captain, sir."

"I'm not one of those antislavery zealots, but I see no reason to risk the future of a boy who put his fate in my hands. You will have enough trouble, Noah, in keeping clear of the slave catchers. Today no one but those on the *Verity* will have heard of you. But within a month ships will have brought newspapers and broadsides listing your name and description. It will not be safe for you in Boston."

The name of the boy they would be seeking would be Michael Lautrec, not Noah Brown. In Boston only Moses knew his former name. But he could not change his appearance. Or his words. These New Englanders spoke differently; their words were clipped and abrupt.

Moses nodded. "I'll be helping him, Captain. He'll stay with me for now." Moses looked at Noah. "The boy's been interested in the District of Maine. I think a vessel headed down east might be a safe place for him."

"Excellent idea, Moses. Excellent. I, too, will make inquiries. For now, take him home and have your wife feed him something other than johnnycake and salt pork."

"Yes, sir," Moses said, smiling. "I'll do that. Are you sure you would not want me with you when you talk with Mrs. Strong?"

"No. It is the job of a captain. If your wife, or perhaps another woman in the area who knows his wife, could stop in later this evening, though, to offer some female comfort?"

"I will make sure of it." Moses turned to go, gesturing that Noah should go with him.

"Thank you, Captain, sir," said Noah again. "Thank you, for everything."

"Just go now," replied the captain as he raised his hand at Jack Strong's door. Noah heard the echo of the knock as he and Moses hurried farther down the street, making several more turns before they arrived at another white door. Here Moses entered without knocking.

"Mrs. Smith, your husband has returned. And he's brought another mouth to feed." Noah had never heard Moses' voice sound so loud and clear. He stood back as his friend was quickly surrounded and embraced by three young women and then by a short, rounded older woman with gray hair and a warm smile who held her husband for several minutes before turning to Noah.

"And who is this young man?" she asked. Without waiting for a response, the woman headed him toward the back of the house, where welcoming smells indicated the kitchen must be. "Whoever he is, he'll be wanting a warm dinner. We've chowder in the pot and corn bread in the oven."

Moses and his family lived in a whole house. Most free blacks in Charleston didn't live in more than a room or two. Noah wasn't sure what chowder was, but it smelled wonderful.

He was in Boston. He was free. And he had friends to help him.

Papa would have said, "You're in high cotton, boy, high cotton." For someone from the South, there was no better place.

Chapter 21

"How'll we get it home?" says Robbin to Bobbin,
"How'll we get it home?" says Bobbin to Robbin,
"How'll we get it home?" says John-all-alone,
"How'll we get it home?" says every one!

—lines from the nineteenth-century Massachusetts
version of a Welsh folk song, "The Hunting of the Wren"

$\mathcal{N}$oah paced back and forth. For two weeks he had been hiding in the attic space above the second floor of Moses' brother's home.

"Ezra Lean is a mean-minded man, and he knows who you are and where I live. It is not safe for you to stay here," Moses had said that first night in Boston. "We must find a place for you to stay until Lean ships out. And until we are sure no advertisements for the runaway Michael Lautrec have been received in Boston."

Noah had a pallet and homespun woolen blanket, a chamber pot, and a jar of water. Someone, usually Moses himself, brought news and food, morning and night. There was a small porthole window in the attic looking out on rooftops and sky, but it was covered with a thin piece of blue gingham. Moses cautioned Noah to stay hidden behind the cloth during the day, when he might be seen by someone in the street below.

"You are not the only former slave hiding in Massachusetts. Although many in this state are against slavery, there are still men who would look to fill their pockets with reward money before they would look to help a runaway."

Two days later Moses reported that several people had seen Ezra Lean and Ben Trader lurking nearby. Lean had made inquiries of several neighbors. Clearly, they were looking for Noah. "Some days I will be the one to bring you food, as I have been doing, but on other days my brother's wife will come, or one of my daughters. I want to be sure no one connects you to this house. Since it is my brother's, I would be likely to visit occasionally. But not twice each day."

Noah put the pallet where he could lie on it and see the sky beyond the cloth covering the window. Some days white clouds floated where he could see them; other days the skies were heavy with a dark gray ceiling. Gulls like those he had seen in Charleston flew by, as did sparrows and pigeons.

Birds could come and go at will.

Perhaps he was free—in Massachusetts slavery was illegal—but he was in an attic space under a roof so steep he could stand up straight only in the center of the room. His pacing followed a short path—six steps one way and six steps back. This attic was more confining than being a slave in Charleston had ever been. He was still dependent on others. Although here he was dependent on a friend, not on a master.

One day Moses brought him twelve pottery marbles and a piece of string. Noah had seen white boys playing with marbles in the gardens of Charleston but had never owned any himself. He practiced with the marbles for hours each day, designing new games and patterns to keep himself amused.

Without those marbles he felt he would have gone mad. Why did Moses think this hiding and waiting necessary? Wasn't Boston a large enough city in which to hide? Moses explained many times that in Boston there were fewer Africans than in Carolina. That those who were not immediately recognized were often questioned. Moses explained, but Noah still wanted to get out of this confined space. To explore the city, to see northern people. His muscles ached for lack of use.

He dreamed of the sea and of open waters and fresh salt air. He had come so far. But not yet far enough.

Every day he asked Moses when he could leave the attic. "I could leave the city. Must be there are other places in Massachusetts."

"Indeed there are other places, if you have someone to find you work and ensure no one asks too many questions." Moses looked at him. "Noah, your words tell people you're from the South. Few free Africans from the South are traveling in New England."

"Then where can I go? Where will I be safe?"

"The District of Maine might be. It is as far north as you can get in the United States. Fewer people live there, and they have more need for strong and willing workers."

"Would they be gettin' the same newspapers and broadsides as Boston?"

"They would. But they get them later and tend not to read

them as closely. Few slave catchers bother to go as far north as Maine. Although that does not keep you safe from any man who feels he could make a few dollars by transporting you to the slavers in Boston." Moses hesitated. "And the District of Maine is closer still to Canada."

"Canada?"

"There you could truly be free; laws protect you from being returned to slavery in the United States."

"Is there no slavery, then, in Canada?"

"Little. And there is land in Canada and a need for laborers. Newcomers are welcome, no matter their color."

Noah thought. "In Canada would there be need for men who know the waters?"

"Much need in the provinces near the North Atlantic. Nova Scotia, Prince Edward Island, Newfoundland—all places with much water and fishing and shipping." Moses looked at Noah, who had pulled a light blanket around his shoulders. Although it was almost June, the day was dank and chilly even in the enclosed attic. "It is frigid cold in Canada. You would soon get your fill of ice and snow there."

Noah shivered. "I be likin' to see Maine. Perhaps there be a place for me there."

"I walk the wharves each day, hoping to hear of any vessel headed down east that could use a crew member. It is best you sail quickly. I would like to see you safely gone before I ship again. And Captain Surridge and the *Verity* leave Thursday for New London and ports south. I am listed to sail with him."

"How many days until Thursday?"

Moses hesitated. "Two."

Two days. "And if no down east vessel willin' to take me by then?"

"Then we will see what other possibilities exist. I will be at sea for perhaps three or four weeks."

That night Noah's head was full of tall ships and far horizons. He dreamed of gulls dropping china dishes onto rocks and laughing as they flew away. He dreamed of being trapped in a world of snow so deep he could not move his legs or arms. He woke clutching his blanket close. He crept to the window and looked up at the full moon.

Mama's voice came back to him. "The moon followed me to America, and it will follow you wherever you go. It will look down at you, and you will never be alone." Noah prayed the way Mama had taught him. He put Papa's small boat on the windowsill for luck. He sat in the window until he could no longer see the moon and the early-morning air was damp with fog. At some point he fell back to sleep, more at ease with himself and with his future.

Chapter 22

Blow, ye winds, heigh-ho!
See all clear yer runnin' gear.
An' blow, me bully-boys, blow!
—from "Blow, Ye Winds," a nineteenth-century sea chantey

Noah was wakened by urgent knocking.

It was Moses. "Good news! I had a message from Captain Surridge early this morning. A vessel from Maine is in port. It carried masts for the French navy through the British blockade and has returned to Boston loaded with French goods. Two of its crew are Massachusetts men and intend to stay here when the ship returns to Maine. Captain Surridge told the captain of your situation, and there is a place for you on the journey to Maine." Moses' smile was wide.

"You done it!" Noah hardly knew how to react. "You done it!"

"Captain Surridge did it. But no matter who made the deal, you are sailing to Maine."

"Maine." Noah thought of the vessel he had seen in for repairs in Charleston. "An' the name of the vessel?"

"The *Annabelle*."

"Bound to what Maine port?"

"A village called Wiscasset, about two days' sailing."

"Wiscasset!" The homeport of the vessel he'd seen in Charleston! Surely it was meant that Wiscasset be his new home. "When she be sailin'?"

"Tomorrow. Today they are unloading the goods for the Boston owner; the rest will return with the *Annabelle* to the owner in Maine. Shall I go and tell Captain Surridge you'll be there?"

Noah could still scarcely believe it. "Please. Yes. No! Let me go with you to thank him."

Moses hesitated. "It is still not safe. When you are so close to leaving, it would be foolish to run the risk."

"Please, Moses. It would be my one time to be seein' Boston. Chances be Lean and Trader wouldn't be findin' me in one day."

Moses was silent.

"Without Capt'n Surridge I would've been sent back to Charleston in chains. I want to tell him I 'preciate his help." Noah meant the words, but he also greatly desired to walk the streets of Boston just one time before sailing northeast again.

"All right. Come with me to my home. We'll go back ways. First we'll find some breakfast for you. Then we'll see Captain Surridge. Most likely you can berth on the *Annabelle* tonight for an early-morning sail. I would have to take you there at some time today in any case."

Noah slipped his boat and marbles into his pocket and was ready to leave in less than a minute.

The grass between the small houses was still damp with fog as they made their way to Moses' home. Inside the kitchen his wife and daughters were cooking and the smell of fresh-baked bread filled the room.

"You've brought Noah so we can wish him safe passage!" Moses' wife gave Noah a hug. "Some beef pie for breakfast and perhaps apple pudding from yesterday's meal?"

"That would be wonderful, ma'am. Thank you." Noah sat where Mrs. Smith indicated, on a bench next to a corner of the wide pine kitchen table. Each of her three daughters was busy; one rolled pie crust, one kneaded bread dough, and the third knit. He recognized Sarah, who was preparing the pie crust. She had brought his meals to him several times. Sarah smiled shyly at Noah as he sat at the other end of the pine table, where she was working. Her sisters giggled.

"Moses tells me you'll be heading down east." Mrs. Smith placed a plate full of pie in front of Noah. "I'm hoping Maine will be right for you. It is hard in these times for a black man to find a safe place where he can make a home."

"I'm hopin' too, ma'am. I's come a long ways."

"And have farther yet to go. Remember that you have friends in Boston. But friends are a beginning. They cannot make your world for you."

"Without Moses, I would still be a slave toting crates on the Charleston docks. I's thankful to him and to Captain Surridge."

"Moses did what was right." She reached over and touched her husband's hand gently. "Sometimes a man has to risk everything to do what is right. Doing that is what makes him a man."

Noah could see Moses was both embarrassed by and proud of his wife's gesture. He wondered if, someday far in the future, any woman would ever look at him that way.

Sarah reached up and pinned her long black braids so they wouldn't get into her dough. "Noah, when you get to Maine, you must write and let us know how you are."

"I don't know writin'. Slaves don't learn things like that."

Noah's wife spoke quickly. "Of course they don't. We should have thought. Well then, you find someone to write for you, you hear? Until you learn to write for yourself."

Sarah smiled at him again and nodded.

Maybe he could learn to write! He had never even considered such a possibility. But Mrs. Smith and Sarah seemed to take for granted that he would. Noah chewed the pie happily. It was warm and delicious. For the first time in days his stomach relaxed. He grinned back at Sarah.

"We'll be thinking of you and wanting to know you're safe. Or, if not, we'll be wanting to know that, too." Mrs. Smith had taken a straw broom and was now sweeping the floor. "You're a hardworking boy, my husband tells me. And it gives me great joy to see one of our people released from that Southern oppression. You keep working hard, but keep your eyes open too. Even in freedom, there are risks."

Noah grinned at her. "You soundin' like my mama."

"Well, mamas everywhere have some things in common. We care about our young folks and their futures." She looked at her daughters and at Noah. "You'll all be living in another world than the one Moses and I struggled in. But as long as our people are still in slavery anywhere, we have a long way to go. Sarah, here, wants to teach school someday. Education can help folks to understand each other more and make better decisions for the future."

"Yes, ma'am." Moses couldn't imagine an African girl like Sarah teaching in a place like Charleston. What would Charleston be like if there were no slavery? How would the white folks manage? Most of them didn't know what it was like to work all day. But here in Boston white folks seemed to work hard. Maybe white folks in Charleston could learn too. Or they could pay the Africans for work done. Let every person decide where to live and what work to do. Noah smiled just thinking about such a world, where every child could go to school.

"Come along, Noah. Finish up that pie. We need to be getting to Captain Surridge and then to the *Annabelle*." Moses pulled on a jacket he'd taken from a peg on the back wall. He then handed another to Noah. "It'll be chilly at sea and on the coast of Maine. You take this old jacket of mine; it will warm you."

Noah stuffed the last of the pie into his mouth and put on the jacket.

It was heavy blue wool, patched with canvas. A seaman's jacket. It fit just right. "Thank you. An' for the food today an' past days. An' for hidin' me."

"You'll thank us by taking care of yourself and by having a fine life." Mrs. Smith gave him one more hug. "Now, Moses, you get this boy safely to his vessel."

Noah took one more look around the warm kitchen. He

wished he'd grown up in a home like this. A home with two parents, where children could feel at ease and where lives could be planned in peace. He hugged Mrs. Smith one more time. He hadn't hugged anyone like that since Mama died.

"Good-bye, Noah," said Sarah.

"I'll learn writin'. I will." Noah wished he could stay. Maybe Sarah could have taught him.

"Come on," Moses said. The two of them left by the back door, making their way through streets and alleys, avoiding major roadways. Noah saw ironsmiths and shoemakers, grocers and tinsmiths, harness makers and tailors. At one school black children played in the yard, and at another white children stood talking. A white boy was crying, "Papers for sale!" in the street. From the number of newspapers he was selling, Noah guessed more people in Boston knew how to read than had in Charleston.

They walked quickly. Noah looked at everything and tried to remember it all.

Soon they came to a more formal part of town. The buildings were larger and the people wore finer clothing. "We are near Captain Surridge's home," Moses confirmed. His house was tall and narrow, and redbrick steps led up to the door. Moses walked right up those front steps without hesitating. A white woman answered his knock.

"We came to see Captain Surridge," said Moses.

"He's left already this morning. Gone down to the *Verity*," she answered.

"Thank you," replied Moses. "We'll seek him there."

They turned down another street and Noah could see beyond them the waters of Boston Harbor.

As they got closer to the waterfront the buildings changed again. Here were the warehouses, taverns, grogshops, sail lofts, and chandleries. Businesses that depended on the seas and on the men who sailed them.

The smells of salt water and mudflats, of tar and new wood and paint, got stronger the closer they got to the wharves. Familiar smells, even though these streets were unfamiliar. But wharves here were not like those in Charleston. Most men here were white.

"We're close now," said Moses, pointing to his right. "The *Verity* lies just beyond that schooner."

Captain Surridge was on deck. "Have you found the *Annabelle* and Captain Dodge?" he asked.

"We're on our way there now," replied Moses. "Noah wanted to thank you."

"Sir, I be wantin' to thank you. If'n you didn't help me . . ." Noah just looked at the captain. "I wisht I could repay you. I thanks you with all my heart."

"You are most welcome, Noah. You become a fair and honest man and a credit to your race, and that will be repayment enough. I've told Captain Dodge you will work well with his crew. Make sure you do so."

"Yes, sir. I swear."

"Now, get yourself over there and off my vessel, or I'll have you polishing brass before the morning is over!"

Noah almost agreed to do so, until he realized the captain was joking. "Yes, sir! Thank you again, sir."

"The *Annabelle*'s a good-size vessel. She sails across the Atlantic once or twice a year, I believe," Moses said as they walked back onto the street and turned right toward a long line of wharves and vessels.

"Get that boy! He's a fugitive!"

The cry came from the open door of a grogshop along the street. Noah recognized the voice immediately. It was Ezra Lean's.

Chapter 23

I an' Satan had a race, Hal-le-lu, hal-le-lu,
I an' Satan had a race, Hal-le-lu-lah.

—from "I an' Satan," a South Carolina spiritual

Moses and Noah ran up one street, circled several shops, and then headed through an alley and back toward the waterfront. Once, Noah heard Lean stumble and swear. But then the footsteps were back. The day was cool, but Moses and Noah were sweating. Their heavy jackets weighed them down.

Several bystanders watched the three men running, but none joined Lean, or offered sanctuary to Moses and Noah. The watchers, in fact, seemed amused by the race.

"Two cents says the white man catches them," said one heavyset man in a shop doorway.

"My money's on the young fellow!" countered a call from an open window.

As the men joked Noah ran for his life.

Where could they go?

Moses knew the waterfront. Noah had to depend on him. So far Moses had been right about everything. Even about the danger in stopping to see Captain Surridge. Would Ezra Lean have seen them if they had gone straight to the *Annabelle*, as Moses had wanted them to?

They dodged a horse cart filled with water barrels. Moses was slowing down. Noah could run faster. But run to where? There had to be a way of stopping Lean.

A high stack of barrels was ahead of them.

"Go near the barrels," Noah gasped.

Moses understood. While Moses ran behind the barrels, Noah ran along the narrow path between them. Ezra Lean was only a few steps behind. Suddenly Noah turned, jumped toward one of the barrels, and with all his strength knocked it toward Lean.

The heavy barrel caught the man unaware and off balance. He threw up his arms and stepped backward, trying to catch himself. "Black devils!"

Noah knocked another barrel toward him and another. Lean caught himself the first time he was hit, but the second barrel knocked him over. As he was pulling himself upright again the third barrel hit him and he fell backward, hitting his head against the cobblestones.

Noah paled. Had he killed the man? A black man who killed a white man, under any circumstances, was doomed.

Quickly Moses stooped down to look at Lean. "He's still breathing. And he smells of rum." The diagnosis was a welcome one. "Anyone finding him here will think he fell down drunk. Unless we are here to blame." Moses stood up. "Get to the *Annabelle*. Quickly. She's anchored two wharves north of here." He pointed. "Introduce yourself to Captain Dodge. Tell him you're grateful and would be happy to assist in preparations for sail, but would prefer to work belowdecks for today. He's talked with Captain Surridge. He won't question you."

"And you?"

"I will take another route and go back to the *Verity*. Trader will be there, but Lean is not sailing with her this trip. Captain Surridge prefers a more peaceful journey than Lean provides. I'll send a message to my wife that I'll not be to home tonight. The *Verity* sails tomorrow, as does the *Annabelle*. We'll both be out of Boston before Lean's head stops aching."

"Thank you, Moses."

"And good luck to you, my friend. May you find fair weather and a place you can stick fast."

"If you should get back to Charleston . . ."

"Then I'll be sure to tell Cudjoe you are in free country and beginning a fine new life there."

Noah hesitated and then hugged the older man.

"Go, then. Before Lean wakens." Moses gave Noah a push, and Noah started running again. Slowly this time. He turned and looked back. Moses was walking in the opposite direction.

Chapter 24

The clouds are high an' steady, the wind is comin' free;
We'll hoist our main t'gans'ls an' speed across the sea.

—from "Home, Dearie, Home," a nineteenth-century sea chantey

The *Annabelle* was a fine ship and the largest vessel Noah had yet sailed on. Southeast winds filled her sails as the *Annabelle* cut through the dark green waters of the northeast seas. The winds blew cold, and Noah was glad of Moses' jacket.

The other crew members, close to home after four months, were full of high spirits and accepted Noah's presence without question. He pulled his weight on the sheets and halyards, did as he was told, was there when needed and shared the thrill of anticipation and relief when a cheer went up from the crew as the *Annabelle* sailed past Seguin Light and headed north into the wide mouth of the Sheepscot River.

"In 1797 George Washington himself ordered that lighthouse set there," said a tall, young seaman next to Noah. "Pretty nigh close to being to home when a Maine man sights Seguin."

"And Wiscasset?" Noah asked.

"Twelve miles upriver." The tall seaman's blond hair was braided in the same sort of queue as Noah's. "I'm Beck Nordstrom. Welcome to the District of Maine!"

Noah smiled. "I's pleased to be here. Mighty pleased."

Rum was broken out, and the officers shared a bottle of French brandy.

Noah hung on to the cap rail and looked at this new land. It was like nothing he had imagined.

The shores were lined with rocks. Some rocks were high and smooth and lightened by the sun; others were dark and jagged. They rose on both sides of the river in defiance of the sea. Land beyond the rocks was covered by towering dark green trees.

This must be the wilderness he'd heard talk of. There was space here, he could see. Space for a person to live. But it was not as welcoming a land as the low plains of South Carolina, with their sheltering palmettos.

Suddenly Noah could feel a change in the crew and in the waters. On the larboard side the rocks were not as high and the tall trees grew down almost to the river's edge. There were whitewashed homes here among the trees.

The *Annabelle* sailed between one large island to larboard and a smaller one to starboard. A cheer went up from the crew. "We're to home!" yelled Beck, throwing his cap into the air. Ahead of them was a wide harbor crowded with vessels.

Noah could see no pettiaugers, but there were canoes and skiffs and dories and a wide assortment of masted vessels. There were wharves, too, crowded with people and small structures. Beyond the wharves the land rose steeply and the hill was covered with houses. Wiscasset was a village cut out of rocks and forests.

Even among the high trees that surrounded it, a white church steeple stood out against the sky. It was not so fine as Saint Michael's, but a church of God dominated the skies here as one had dominated the skies of Charleston.

"Say, Noah, do you have a place to stay?"

Noah turned to Beck. "Don't know no one here."

"Then, you'll come to home with me. My mother runs a boardinghouse for mariners and other travelers." Beck grinned.

"I's got no money."

"Few of us do. We've not yet been paid for the voyage. I'll talk with Ma about it. You'll get work here, if you want it."

"I be lookin'. I be lookin' to stay."

"Summer months are the time to be in the District of Maine, for sure. And you won't find a prettier village than Wiscasset to spend your money in!"

The two young men smiled at each other as they helped to lower the longboats. After four months at sea far from home Captain Dodge had told everyone they were free to go. The *Annabelle* was large enough and full enough of fine French goods to be safer in the channel, so they anchored there for the night. Unloading would come in the morning.

Families who had seen the *Annabelle*'s arrival were waiting on the wharf. Noah stood to the side and watched his crew-mates be swallowed up by welcoming family and friends.

Wives, mothers, sweethearts, children—it seemed everyone in Wiscasset who had a man on the *Annabelle* had reached the wharf before the men themselves.

"Come on, Noah. This is my mother."

The words were hardly out of Beck's mouth when Noah felt himself almost smothered by a large woman with the same wide smile as her son's. Her long white hair was also braided, but hers was fastened on the top of her head and covered by a plain blue cloth bonnet. "Beck tells me you're mates and you have no place to stay. Of course, you must stay with us. There is space and you'll pay when you can."

"I'd be much obliged." Noah looked at the many vessels in the harbor. There did not appear to be any lighter ships, as in Charleston. He would have to find another sort of job here. "I'll be lookin' for work."

"Ayuh. You can sail and I'll wager you can fish."

Noah nodded.

"What else can you do?"

"Use a hammer. And cook." Noah tried to think of everything he had done.

"Then you'll have no worry about finding a job in Wiscasset. The town's in need of young men. We lost too many to the smallpox this spring." Mrs. Nordstrom shook her head sadly.

Noah understood. The pox was dreaded everywhere. In Charleston, Africans who showed scars proving they had survived smallpox fetched higher prices than those who had not had the disease.

Mrs. Nordstrom looked closely at Noah. "There's always work on fishing boats, and Eben Whittier's tavern is in need of a cook. No reason you couldn't do both, if you'd a mind. Most folks do a variety of things to survive here. Some would say it's a hard land to live in. But it's full of opportunity for a young man with energy."

"Ma is the town midwife, as well as running a boarding-house and making blueberry preserves to sell." Beck grinned at his mother. "She's a real Mainer. Lets no thing nor moment go to waste."

"Waste not, want not. As it should be." The wide woman headed Beck and Noah through the crowds, down the wharf, and toward the street that paralleled the waterfront. "For now, you come back with my Beck, get yourself settled, and take some time to look over the town. Supper will be in two hours, and if you'd like a cup of tea while you're waiting, it'll be ready for you."

The roads were dirt and the houses narrow. There were hardly more than a dozen streets in town. Much as he looked, Noah saw no one of his color.

They walked only a few blocks before they reached the graying clapboard boardinghouse. It stood right on the street with no fence and no garden to speak of. Beyond there was a wide field, and to the right a mudflat where the Sheepscot waters had receded with the tide. Only a few marsh grasses covered the expanse of dark mud. In Charleston the flat would have been green with grasses.

But here there were no chains or shackles.

Here all men and women appeared to work for what they got. Noah could do that.

He looked over the Sheepscot River at the *Annabelle* and the other vessels anchored there. For a small village, there were a large number of vessels. That promised a good future. Each of those vessels would need to be crewed.

Out on the mudflat a blue heron searched for crabs and minnows in tide pools.

"Noah! Come and taste Ma's bread with her blueberry preserves!" Beck called out. "There's nothing like this at sea."

Noah smiled to himself and headed inside.

Chapter 25

I'll sing to you of the good old times,
When people were honest and true . . .
When every man was a working man
and earned his livelihood,
And women were smart and industrious
and lived for their family's good.

—from "Old Pod-Auger Times,"
a nineteenth-century New England folk song

*M*rs. Nordstrom had been right. Noah had no trouble finding work in Wiscasset. After he helped unload the *Annabelle*, he found several other vessels that could use extra hands for loading or unloading.

Then he asked directions to Eben Whittier's tavern.

"Boy! You looking for me?"

Mr. Whittier was stooped and white-haired. He reminded Noah of an angry old man who had sometimes attended Saint Michael's and was too quick with the lash. Noah started to back out of the tavern door. Mr. Whittier beckoned him back in.

"I's Noah Brown. I heared you was lookin' for a cook."

"Are you a cook?"

"My mama was cook in a big house in Charleston. I learned some from her. An' I cooked on a brig comin' north."

Mr. Whittier looked him up and down and then clapped him on the shoulder. "Well, your cooking can't be worse than mine. Mrs. Greenleaf!"

A short, rounded white woman came through a door in the back of the tavern room, wiping her hands on her yellow calico apron. "Mrs. Greenleaf, this young fellow is Noah Brown, and he says he can cook. Show him where the fire is and let's see what he can do."

Mrs. Greenleaf looked at Noah askance, but after she tasted his lobster pie, which substituted lobster for the shrimp Mama had used, she was won over. "Fruit pies and meat pies are common enough, but it took a black boy to show me fish pies," she exclaimed over her third generous helping. In exchange she showed Noah how to make the heavy stews filled with potatoes and beef or pork that were the usual Wiscasset tavern fare.

They soon worked out a schedule. Mrs. Greenleaf did the cooking during the day while Noah worked as he was needed on the waterfront. Mr. Whittier was also the Wiscasset post-master, and during the day women or children would often stop at the tavern for mail or messages. Mrs. Greenleaf ensured that small sweet cakes were always on hand, and lemonade and tea as available as stronger drinks. In the evenings, however, when the tavern patrons were men and the odors of spirits and tobacco took over the room, Mr. Whittier trusted the kitchen to Noah. The old man would rather debate President Thomas Jefferson's trade policies over a brandy than worry about what was happening in the kitchen. Noah ensured that the customers were well cared for. He chopped and baked and introduced seasoned Carolina rice and spicy crab gumbo to Wiscasset.

He soon discovered there were other African Americans in Wiscasset. Two old men and one woman who had been household slaves before freedom came to the District of Maine in 1783 had stayed on as paid servants to the families they served. And several younger black families were headed by men who were mariners.

John Bascomb was one, and he and Noah became friends. John and his wife, Sophie, had moved to Wiscasset from Connecticut, hoping for more opportunities on the frontier. They lived in a few rooms over Payson's Wharf, but they also owned land outside of the village, where they grew vegetables and planned someday to build a house.

Sally and Joseph, the Bascomb children, were cherished openly, since their precious Willy had died earlier that spring in the smallpox epidemic. Noah showed Joseph how to play marbles and spent Sunday evenings, when the tavern was closed, talking with John and Sophie.

"I've dreamed of bein' a mariner," Noah confided. "But mariners be seldom to home." Sally sat happily on his lap, playing with strands of hair from his long queue. "Someday mebbe I'd be wantin' a family like yours. A job close to home might be best."

"There are many ways to earn a living without being absent for long periods," John suggested. "The coaster I crew on makes weekly trips to Portland, but each trip is only four days. I'm gone but half the month."

Two weeks away out of four was not bad. Deepwater mariners were away for months at a time. "I'm thinkin' of fishin'. Could a living be made fishin' Maine waters?"

"Ayuh. Men in Wiscasset fish for their families, not for profit. But downriver and on the coastal islands, like Monhegan, men fish for a living."

"How far to sea would a man have to sail to pull in enough fish to support a family?"

"Not far. The Gulf of Maine is deep and nets of fish are for the taking. But waters and winds are high and currents strong. You'd be needing a fair-size vessel and a crew."

"An' the Canada Banks? I heard tell cod be thick there."

"True enough. But you'd need a larger vessel to go the distance. And the Banks can be fished with some safety only in summer. Fall and winter storms have sunk many a vessel. Not that weather stops men from as far away as England or France from fishing there."

"An' what would the cost be of ownin' such a fishing vessel?" Noah thought of Papa's small fishing boat. No crew had been needed, and Papa had fished the Carolina Sea Islands during the day and spent the night on his own pallet on land twelve months of the year.

"I'd say two or three years' wages if you're frugal and start with a small craft. There are shipbuilders who might give you credit in return for a share of the catch once they know you. It's been done."

Joseph tugged at Noah's shirt. "Please, Noah, one more game of marbles? Please?"

Noah put Sally down and made a circle on the floor with

a piece of string. "Now, you take these six marbles and I'll take the other six. We'll see who wins the most!"

"Me! I will!" declared Joseph as his father and mother laughed.

Noah had soon saved a small cache of coins, which joined his boat and his marbles under the pallet in the room he shared with up to three other men in need of a night's lodging.

He first paid Mrs. Nordstrom for a month's room. "Be sure to think toward wintering, Noah," she advised, tucking his coins into the pocket hanging around her waist. "When there's a good northeast blow, you'll be needing warmer clothes for sure and thick leather boots."

"My jacket is warm." Noah was proud of the jacket Moses had given him.

"It is a good jacket for autumn, but in winter you'll be needing a heavy wool shirt under it and a hat and gloves. And the trousers you're wearing won't warm you. You'll need heavier ones."

"I have money."

"Ayuh, and you're working long enough hours to be adding to it. But in the winter few vessels sail and few visitors come to Wiscasset. You'd best have enough saved to get you through months with little work."

In Charleston he had needed few clothes, and any that were needed he'd been given by Mrs. Lautrec. "There be many needs in this Maine."

Mrs. Nordstrom nodded. "Indeed there are. But you'll be fine." She looked him over. "You'll be needing wool stockings, too, to keep your feet warm and dry. I've knit more stockings in my life than I care to think of. I'd be glad to knit you a pair or two, if you wouldn't mind."

Noah smiled. "No, ma'am. I sure wouldn't be mindin'. Thank you!"

Mariners came and went from the boardinghouse. But Beck was always there. Sometimes Beck asked Noah to join him and other young men in Wiscasset in some activity.

"We're just going to play some cards and have a little rum," Beck urged one night. "Come with us! You're too serious!"

"I have to be gettin' to the tavern," Noah replied. "I have a job to do."

"Mr. Whittier can do without you for one night. You're young—you shouldn't work all the time. Have some fun!"

Noah just shook his head. Beck did not have to pay for his room and board, and had no need to plan ahead further than this evening. Like most mariners, he would spend his money, and when the money was gone, he would ship out again.

Noah would not allow himself to be so careless. He watched and listened and saved every cent he could, as Mrs. Nordstrom had advised. Maybe someday he would even own a fishing boat. But he did envy Beck his friends and looked forward to Sunday evenings with John and Sophie.

And he made one other friend.

One morning shortly after he arrived in Wiscasset, Noah saw a small, red-haired boy racing up and down the wharves, tugging on people's clothing, apparently asking questions.

When the boy got to where Noah was standing, he stopped again.

"Please, sir," the boy said very seriously, "please, have you seen my pa?"

"What be your pa's name?" Noah asked, amused at being called "sir" by a white boy and at the thick red curls that covered this boy's head. He had seen small black children with that many curls, but few white children. And none with hair as bright red as this boy's.

"I'm Seth Chambers. He's Stephen Chambers. He's a mariner. Everyone knows him."

"Well, I be new here. I have not met him."

"He's very tall and very brave," Seth said earnestly. "And he's been gone a very long time. He's been gone since I was three."

"And how old are you now, Seth Chambers?"

The boy stood up very straight and tried to stand on his toes to make himself look even taller. "I am four, of course."

"Of course." Noah smiled. "I can see that."

"How old are you?"

"I be fourteen."

"That's old. My pa sailed on the *Fame*. Last fall."

The *Fame*. The ship Noah had seen in Charleston that had run aground on Charleston Bar and needed repairs.

"Seth Chambers, why did you run off again?" A flushed, brown-haired girl who had just run up to them took Seth's arm and started to pull him away. Clearly she was his older sister. Her long, thick hair, which earlier must have been pinned up, had fallen. "Why didn't you stay in the yard as I told you? I have work to do for Widow Chase, and I'll not have my chores finished for looking for you."

"I seen your papa's ship." Noah told them about the damaged ship in Charleston Harbor. But he had no way of knowing where their father was.

After that Noah kept his eyes open for the small, determined boy. Too often Seth would escape from the home where he and his sister lived and come searching for his absent father on the docks. Noah was angry with Seth's father. He had been gone too long without word. Seth's worry and need for his father was one more reason Noah wanted to work the seas but not be away from home for long. He vowed his son would never have to wander the docks looking for him.

"I saw you with Seth Chambers yesterday," Sophie said one Sunday. "He used to play on the docks with our Willy." Sophie dabbed her eyes with her apron. "That smallpox that took Willy took Seth's ma, too. Now his sister works for the Widow Chase, whose husband died of the pox and left her with a baby coming. It was crying times here in the spring."

Noah knew how it felt to be alone and to have to depend on yourself. Seth and his sister, Abbie, were white, but they were responsible for their future, as Noah was. Whenever Noah saw Seth wandering the wharves, he took his hand and returned him to his sister.

One night as Noah walked back to Mrs. Nordstrom's after the tavern closed he saw tiny flickers of light in the air, like floating candles. As a boy he had chased lights like those in the garden at Tradd Street. Noah quickly looked around. No one else was in the street. He ran down Main Street, laughing with delight, chasing the fireflies. Holding them gently in clasped hands held high above his head, he walked to the river, watching their light flicker through the spaces between his fingers like tiny beacons.

"You made a home for you'selves here in this north

country of pine trees and dark waters. If creatures as small as you can do that, then so can I." Noah opened his hands and released them.

They flew off, out toward moonlight reflected in the waters of the Sheepscot.

Noah's steps bounced a bit as he walked back along the dirt street toward the boardinghouse. Somehow tonight he didn't feel so lonely.

Chapter 26

Satan tell me to my face, Hal-le-lu, hal-le-lu,
He will break my kingdom down, Hal-le-lu, hal-le-lu.
—from "I an' Satan Had a Race," a South Carolina spiritual

*M*ost nights when he got to the tavern, Noah found Mrs. Greenleaf had left a half dozen loaves of bread and an assortment of pies she had made during the day. It did not take long to make the stews or cook the seafood the men wanted with their rum or cider. There was no one in the kitchen to socialize with. Once he borrowed a book from Mr. Whittier's cabinet, thinking perhaps he could teach himself to read, but the book was thick and filled with tiny black marks he could make no sense of. Perhaps if there were someone to teach him. But there was no one.

So Noah amused himself in the long evenings of summer and early fall by sitting next to the half-opened kitchen door and listening to the men who patronized the tavern.

He heard talk of the British, who were not allowing other countries to trade with France, and of a general called Napoléon who seemed to be at war with everyone. Men spoke disparagingly of President Jefferson for not objecting more to British attempts to prevent Americans from trading in the West Indies. They complained that legislators in Boston had no understanding of boundary issues in the District of Maine. The silversmith, Mr. Dole, had just hired a Mr. Mead to assist him in the making of clocks. Young Michael Quinn's wife, Rachel, was in the family way.

Night after night the words were the same, even if the words and speakers differed.

By early October leaves were turning red and yellow and orange. Hills around Wiscasset and across the Sheepscot looked like quietly changing firework displays. Noah wore Moses' coat most days now and was glad of the stockings Mrs. Nordstrom had knit him and the pair of moose-leather boots he had ordered from the shoemaker. There was no snow as yet, but, "Just wait," promised Mrs. Nordstrom as she started another pair of stockings. "Just you wait. Cold and snow will be here soon enough."

It was a Monday night, usually one of the quieter evenings at the tavern, and Noah had dozed off next to the heat of the kitchen stove, when he suddenly heard someone say "Charleston."

Talk of the South was not common in Wiscasset. Noah was immediately alert. He opened the door to the main tavern room farther so he could see who was speaking.

"Those cotton plantations outside of Charleston need an

unending supply of slaves to keep them profitable. Tobacco planters in Virginia and Maryland are selling many of their slaves south; tobacco growing isn't going well, and many feel slavery won't last much longer. They want to sell their property while they can. The highest prices for slaves are in South Carolina now." The man talking was a stranger to Noah, a brawny, black-haired man smoking a long clay pipe.

Mr. Whittier shook his head. "Slavery is not a pretty business. It would be just as well if it disappeared. Faded, somehow, into a quaint custom of the past. In Massachusetts and here in the District of Maine we had no trouble outlawing it."

"Easy enough for Massachusetts and Maine. There were only a few slaves here. The Carolinas are full of them. In Charleston there are more black faces in the streets than white. Planters have their fortunes tied up in land and slaves. Without slaves there would be no cotton plantations. And no Southern fortunes made off them." The stranger took another long drink of rum from his tankard.

Mr. Whittier continued. "Ayuh. I suppose so. It's the way of things today, as you say. But not forever. The men at the Constitutional Convention saw that. That's why they set the 1808 deadline for importing slaves."

"And to beat the deadline, slave ships fill Charleston Harbor. Men are offering high prices for trained slaves. Even runaways who can't be trusted can be returned by anyone who finds them, for a high amount."

"I'd think they'd rather buy a new slave than spend the time to find a runaway," Mr. Whittier commented.

"It's the principle of the thing. They want to show slaves how stealing the master's property is punished. Why, finding escaped slaves and returning them is a regular profession now. Philadelphia, New York, Providence, Boston—they're all full of escaped slaves. Trouble is, the freed ones are hiding the runaways, and it's hard to find them. At least that's something I wouldn't think you'd see much of in Wiscasset—an escaped slave! Can you imagine a Southern-speaking black person on the banks of the Sheepscot?"

Noah didn't wait to hear the answer. He was now known in town. Although no one had ever asked about his past, he had spoken with Beck and Mrs. Nordstrom of his escape, and, as Moses had warned him, his accent was one of the South. Anyone listening in that room could easily draw the correct conclusion: Indeed, there was an escaped slave in Wiscasset. And money to be made by returning him. Noah couldn't take a chance.

He carefully opened the kitchen door of the tavern, stepped outside, and closed it silently behind him. The sun was setting earlier each night; Main Street was dim in the twilight. His body wanted to run, but running would call attention to himself. He walked near the walls of the stores on Main Street.

He had to talk with someone. John was at sea, and he didn't want to worry Sophie and the children. Who else could he trust?

Walking the three blocks to Mrs. Nordstrom's seemed to take three hours.

She was in the kitchen, cleaning up from the evening's supper.

"Did Eben close the tavern early tonight?"

"No." Noah hesitated. She was a white woman. But she

reminded him of Mama. She might be able to help. Although how, he could not imagine.

"There be a man from away at the tavern. He talkin' of slaves runnin' and the money men in Charleston would pay to those who would be bringin' 'em back. People were listenin'. Men here know the sound of my talkin' is of the South."

"Sit down, Noah." Mrs. Nordstrom sat on one of the benches, polishing a pewter bowl with a soft cloth. "You knew this might happen."

"I hopin' not."

"Of course you were. Was anything said about you in particular?"

Noah shook his head. "I was too afeared to stay. But I felt they were talkin' 'bout me."

"No doubt they were. You and others." Mrs. Nordstrom sat and stared into the bowl. Finally she looked up at Noah. "You know Wiscasset is not a safe place for you now. People know you live here. It is time for you to move on."

"But to where?"

"Somewhere far. Somewhere no one talks of the South and of slaves. Somewhere there is no reward money for anyone who would take you back."

Noah looked at her. "That only be Canada."

She sighed. "It does. It's the one truly safe place."

"Then, I have to leave." Noah's voice was low.

"I'm sorry to say it, you know." Mrs. Nordstrom put down the bowl and went over to where Noah sat. She put her hands on his shoulders. "I should like you to stay, Noah. You're a hardworking young man, and you'll make a success of whatever life you decide is right for you. But you have to be in a safe place to make that life."

"How might I be gettin' to Canada?"

Mrs. Nordstrom walked over to the window and looked out at the street. "Not through the woods, for sure. It's too late in the year and too many dangers are there. Trails, such as they are, are hard to find in the best of weather." She turned around. "It must be by sea."

"No one be sailin' to Canada from Wiscasset 'cept fishermen headin' for the Grand Banks." Noah thought a moment. "That's what I got to do, isn't it? I got to find a fisherman who will take me."

Mrs. Nordstrom frowned a bit. "It's late in the year for voyages to the Banks. Few risk October storms. But down at Mrs. Brewer's—she's the one I assisted to have a fine baby daughter just two days ago—I heard her father-in-law was sailing to Nova Scotia this week. He was waiting until the baby was well born and then was heading out. I remember, for she was concerned. Seas are heavy this time of year."

"Where could I be findin' him?"

"This time of night he'd perhaps be at his son's home. Fourth house from Main on Middle Street."

Noah turned to go.

"Tell him I sent you. And that you're skilled at seafaring. I suspect Mr. Brewer could use a hand. Few will want to sail northeast this late in the year."

Noah nodded and looked at her again. "Thank you."

"There's no time for that now. Thank me when you're gone and safe."

Chapter 27

A land of promise there ye'll see,
I'm bound away across that sea.

—from "Across the Western Ocean,"
a nineteenth-century sea chantey

*A*mos Brewer was glad of another hand to help him in deep seas. Noah had been afraid he might have to use his carefully saved hoard of coins to pay for his passage, but instead Mr. Brewer offered to let him work for it.

"I'd want to be stayin', then, in that Canada."

"No problem for me, son. I'm carrying rum and molasses to Lunenberg. No reason you couldn't stop there. But you must understand it will be a dangerous journey. It is too late to fish the Banks, and this will be a brief trip. I hope to be back in Wiscasset before November."

"Be there men who work the seas in Lunenberg?"

"Ayuh. Many. Most live by fishing, although there are

140

shipbuilders and mariners of different sorts. Vessels from Europe, too, stop at Lunenberg for supplies when they're fishing the Grand Banks." Mr. Brewer took his pipe out of his mouth and knocked the ashes onto the floor, to the obvious aggravation of his daughter-in-law, lying with her new baby on a pallet near the fire. "I've seen men of your color there too. Should that be of interest to you."

"Yes, sir." Noah grinned. "It is. Lunenberg is soundin' like a fine place."

"It's part of Nova Scotia," said Mr. Brewer. "So it's not so far north as some Canadian places. But it'll be plenty cold out on the water this time of year, and on land, too. You have some warm clothes, I hope?"

"Boots and stockings. And a seaman's coat." Noah was proud of them all.

"You'll be needing more than that." He looked over at his daughter-in-law, who nodded at him. "I'll look about and see if we can't find you some gloves and perhaps a wool shirt. My son and I have more clothes than we can wear in a day, and have some for Sundays left over besides."

"Thank you, sir. I'd 'preciate that," Noah said gratefully.

"I'll check tonight. You have your gear on the *Emma* tomorrow morning. It's tied at Johnston's Wharf, where the channel is deep. There'll be five of us sailing. We'll leave on the high tide tomorrow afternoon."

Noah nodded.

"Do you have a place to stay until then?"

"I be staying at Mrs. Nordstrom's."

"You should be fine, then." Mr. Brewer looked at him. "I've heard of no vessels sailing south tomorrow."

Mr. Brewer knew, then. He knew of Noah's danger. "Thank you again, sir."

"You're likely and you're known. No reason for you not to have a life of your own making. Most of us came here, or our fathers or grandfathers came here, so we could make our own lives. Seems to me every man should have the right to do that."

"Yes, sir." Noah backed toward the door. "I be seein' you in the morning, then. The *Emma*. At Johnston's Wharf. And thank you, sir!"

By the time he had gotten back to Mrs. Nordstrom's, she had gone through her husband's clothes. He had died at sea several years before.

"I never wanted to cut this fabric and the garments were too small for Beck. But my husband would have been proud to see them worn by a young mariner."

Noah looked with amazement, and some embarrassment, as Mrs. Nordstrom handed him two pairs of flannel drawers and an underwaistcoat, to wear under his shirt. And then he laughed as she handed him two small knit hats. One was a navy-colored knit that he knew could be pulled down to cover his ears and his head. He had seen mariners on the wharves wear sea caps like that one, even this early in the winter. But the other one was gray and much softer and longer. "For what would one wear this hat?" he asked.

"Said only by one who's never known a Canadian winter. Or one in the District of Maine, for that matter. It's a night-cap, Noah, to be worn to bed, to keep your brains from freezing in the night." Mrs. Nordstrom handed him the whole pile. "Now, you go and righten up your things and pack them in this old canvas seabag no one is finding a use for. I'll heat you some water so you can wash up. You'll at least start your journey clean. Heaven knows you won't be long on the seas before you'll smell of more than the fish in those deep waters. But so will you all, so no harm done."

Noah thanked her, took the clothing, and went up to his room to pack. Even after assuring that his possessions were in order, and scrubbing himself as well as he could in the cool evening, he slept little that night. Every time the wind shook the shutters, he was sure it was someone approaching to capture him. When a mouse skittered across the floor, he thought someone was tiptoeing toward his room. He was the only one sleeping there now, so he moved his pallet to block the door. Still, the night was a long one.

It was early when he got up. He put his bag of coins in the pocket of his trousers. It was heavy and awkward, but it wouldn't be tempting to anyone. He trusted Mr. Brewer, but until they were at sea Noah wanted his money near at hand. He kept Papa's boat and his marbles in his inside jacket pocket.

Mrs. Nordstrom insisted on making him a breakfast of pie and coffee.

"Beck is still to bed, so you might as well take a second piece of pie. If Amos Brewer isn't sailing till high tide, it's best you leave your belongings with him, as he suggested, and return here. It will be a long enough day. Better you not spend it out on the wharves, where someone might get an idea you'd rather they not have."

Noah nodded. As he walked along Water Street toward Johnston's Wharf his heavy coin pouch hit his leg with every step. Wiscasset had been a good place for him. He wished he could stay longer. Suddenly he heard his name called.

"Noah! Noah!" Seth Chambers, red curls bouncing, was racing down the hill toward him. "I found you!" Seth looked up at Noah and caught his breath. "I wanted to find you."

"Why, Seth? I's thinkin' you should be in school."

"I'm going to be a mariner. A deep-sea mariner. Like you. Like my pa was. I'm going to sail deep waters."

All in Wiscasset knew word of Seth's pa had finally come. His father was not returning. He had drowned while resisting being impressed.

"Where are you going? You have a seabag. My pa had a seabag. Are you sailing today? Are you going to blue water?" The boy tugged at his arm. "Noah, where are you going?"

"I'm goin' to sail on a fishing vessel to a city in Nova Scotia. In Canada."

"Today? Are you leaving today?"

"I am."

"I'll go with you! I can be a mariner too!"

Noah kept walking. He liked Seth, but having the boy with him did not help to keep his plans quiet. "Shush, Seth. You may be walkin' with me. But you can't be sailin' with me."

"Why not?"

"You are not tall enough yet," said Noah. "To work the ropes you must be taller. You must wait a few years."

"Years! I can't wait years!" Seth chattered and walked with him as Noah headed toward Johnston's Wharf.

"Abbie would be grievin' for you if you went to sea," Noah said. "She be needin' you to help take care of her. An' Widow Chase."

"Abbie doesn't need anyone," said Seth quickly. "She spends all her time with Widow Chase. Just because there's going to be a baby. She doesn't have time for me anymore."

"She loves you."

"Maybe she loves me. She made me a coat for my birthday, Noah. And Widow Chase made me a waistcoat with a ship on it. Did you know I am five now, Noah? I had a birthday. I had cakes, too. Just for me."

"Abbie and Widow Chase sound mighty fond of you."

"Maybe. But I don't need to go to school anymore. If you go to sea, you don't need to read or write, do you?"

"I don't know readin' or writin'. But I wish I did," Noah replied. They were almost to the wharf. "I wish I'd gone to school."

"Why didn't you go, then?" Seth asked.

"'Cause where I was livin' when I be five, there wasn't no schools for me." As they came up to the *Emma*, Noah saw Mr. Brewer and another man. "Good mornin', sir. I's brought my gear."

"Stow it below. Jonathan here will show you where. This is Noah Brown, Jonathan, who I told you was sailing with us."

"Pleased to meet you," said Jonathan, looking at Seth. "Who's the little whippersnapper?"

"I'm Seth Chambers, and I'm not little and I'm going to be a deepwater mariner."

"Well, well, Seth Chambers," Mr. Brewer said. "That sounds like a good goal to work toward. When will you be starting this life as a mariner?"

"Today. I'm going with Noah to Canada." With that, Seth took a big step from the dock onto the deck of the *Emma*.

"Oh, no you're not," said Noah quickly. "Seth'll be returnin' straight home to his sister."

"No! I don't want to go home! I want to sail with you. I could help you, Noah. You're my friend."

"I be your friend, Seth, truly, but sometimes friends be doin' different things. Today is a day for me to sail with Mr. Brewer. A day when you should be in school."

Seth stood with his head down, ignoring the smiles of the two fishermen on the deck. Noah stowed his gear below, as they directed.

"You'll remember we sail on the tide this afternoon," Mr. Brewer reminded him.

"I'll be here," Noah promised. "Alone. Come, Seth. Let's go to Mrs. Nordstrom's. That's where I been livin'. Wouldn't you like to see where mariners live?"

Seth nodded.

"Mebbe Mrs. Nordstrom could find you a piece of pie for breakfast."

"I like pie." Seth brightened. "My sister, Abbie, makes pie. I had some for breakfast. But I can always eat more."

"I guess you can," said Noah as the two of them headed back up Water Street. "I guess you could eat two pieces of pie if you were wantin' to."

"Three. Four! Five!" His attention now on pie rather than on sailing, Seth skipped next to Noah back up Water Street.

Seth's presence made the long day shorter. He had his pie, and more, and chattered on. Noah tried to get Seth to rest and took him to the second-floor room where there were four pallets. But every five minutes Seth had "just one more" question.

It was a relief when Abbie arrived to take him home.

"Have you any idea of how worried I've been?" Abbie was wet from rain and her hair was hanging loosely, as it often was by the time she found Seth.

Noah was glad she had come; she would ensure Seth's return home.

"You'll help Seth to know why I be leavin'," Noah explained to Abbie. "He doesn't know what life be like for someone my color."

Abbie nodded. "I will try to explain. But he will miss you."

Noah gave Seth a big hug. He hugged Mrs. Nordstrom, too.

"Be well, Noah. Get word back to us when you are safe."

"Yes, ma'am. I be doin' that. Soon as I can," he promised. He left the doorway, walking a little faster than necessary, both because of the rain and to ensure that Seth did not follow him. He heard Seth's call of "Good-bye, Noah!" following him as he headed for Johnston's Wharf. He had one more stop to make. He wanted to say good-bye to the Bascombs.

"Noah! Can we play marbles?" Joseph tried to tug Noah to the floor.

"Joseph," he said, reaching deep into his pocket, "I can't be playin' with you today. I have to go away. But you take these marbles, to 'member me by."

After he explained, Sophie hugged him and insisted on giving him the bread she had just baked. "For your journey. Go in safety."

As soon as he arrived at Johnston's Wharf, the *Emma* shoved off. Noah stood on the deck and watched the buildings of Wiscasset vanish in the rainy mist and then the church steeple and then, finally, the vessels in the harbor. He would never be back, as long as there was slavery in this country.

Once again he was leaving good friends to start over. He blinked back the tears and felt in his pocket for his small fishing boat.

As the *Emma* moved down the Sheepscot the clouds began to break. Noah could see the early moon over the trees.

Chapter 28

The following spring a fishing vessel returning from an early trip to the Grand Banks brought back this letter to Wiscasset:

April 1807

Dear Mrs. Nordstrom,

My teacher is helping me write this. Tell Beck and Seth and Abbie and the Bascombs I am well and safe in Canada.

I now live in the city of Lunenberg. I live with two men of my color who are fishermen. I fish with them, and go to school when seas are high and there is snow and ice. I am saving to buy my own fishing boat.

I have a life here. It is a place with a future for me.
Tell Seth he can visit when he is tall and learns the ropes.
I send best wishes.

Your friend,

Noah Brown—a Free Man

P.S. The moon shines in Canada, too.

Historical Notes

*A*lthough the characters in *Seaward Born* are fictional, the world they live in was real. The hurricane of 1804 was one of the most devastating in Charleston's history, and yet many buildings Michael/Noah knows, such as Saint Michael's Episcopal Church and the Exchange, still stand.

The city of Charleston was built on a low, narrow peninsula between the Ashley and Cooper Rivers. Its large, almost landlocked harbor made it a major port in the southern United States during the eighteenth and nineteenth centuries. Nearby rice and indigo fields and, after Eli Whitney's 1793 invention of the cotton gin, cotton plantations made Charleston a leading center of wealth and culture in the southern United States, and the fifth largest city, after New York, Philadelphia, Baltimore, and Boston.

Slavery made that wealth possible.

There were black slaves in Charleston from its beginning and for many years there were more black Americans in South Carolina than there were white. Black slaves worked the rice, indigo, and cotton plantations, built the elegant city, and provided most services, skilled and unskilled, needed by its citizens.

Charleston was the largest port of entry for African slaves sold into what is now the United States. Historian Peter Woods suggests that "the colonial ancestors of present-day Afro-Americans are more likely to have first confronted North America at Charleston than at any other port of entry." Forty percent of African slaves arriving in North America between 1700 and 1775 came to South Carolina, almost all of them through Charleston. And from 1782 until 1808, when the United States Constitution prohibited the importing of people to be slaves, another ninety thousand Africans were brought to Charleston to meet the growing needs of the cotton fields.

Africans brought with them across the Atlantic knowledge of the cultivation and use of rice, skill in building and piloting boats, expertise in crafts, and religious and social beliefs that became interwoven with the culture in which they now found themselves.

Seventeenth- to early-nineteenth-century South Carolina rice plantations were very different from plantations in other areas of the south. Slaves were brought from Gambia specifically because they knew how to cultivate rice. Their white masters, many French in origin, did not. Because of that, Africans in South Carolina were given some independence, and some even attained a degree of power. Some overseers were black. Black slaves designed elaborate irrigation systems for rice fields and then supervised their construction. Most important, economically and socially, many slaves worked on the "task system": They were given work to do for the day, and when that work was completed, they could work for themselves. Some cultivated their own gardens in the slave areas of plantations, some fished the rivers, and some developed skills such as pottery making and basket weaving. They then brought their products to the streets of Charleston to sell. As a result, until the early nineteenth century slaves in South Carolina were more likely than their counterparts in other states to have their own money, to sometimes be able to buy themselves, and to feel as though they were contributing members of society.

This ended in the first and second decades of the nineteenth century as the growing independence of blacks in the Caribbean and in South Carolina made white masters fear their power. The change from rice to cotton plantations also ended the special value Gambians had because of their knowledge of rice cultivation.

In the late eighteenth and early nineteenth centuries about 9 percent of South Carolina's skilled slaves were mariners; they made up 25 percent of the skilled runaways. Thousands of Northern free African Americans worked on the seas. For more information on this major chapter in African American history, see W. Jeffrey Bolster's excellent book *Black Jacks: African American Seamen in the Age of Sail*, listed in the bibliography.

In 1806 the District of Maine was part of Massachusetts. Massachusetts had outlawed slavery in 1783. Although slavery was not allowed there, state laws did honor the federal Fugitive Slave Law, which permitted runaway slaves to be captured and returned to their owners much as other stolen property would be.

Canada was a part of the British Empire, which did not outlaw slavery until 1833, but the institution was never highly regarded or widely accepted in Canada, and many free blacks lived there. Canadian laws prohibited American slave catchers from following former slaves across national borders, so reaching Canada was a goal for many American slaves seeking freedom.

In the early nineteenth century several communities of Africans existed in the Canadian maritime province of Nova Scotia. More than three thousand African Americans who had been slaves in the United States and were British sympathizers during the American Revolution had been relocated to Nova Scotia by the English when the British occupation ended. White Americans who were sympathizers were also relocated to the province, and more than one thousand of them brought Africans as part of their household. David George, a black Baptist pastor originally from South Carolina, founded chapels throughout Nova Scotia during the 1780s and 1790s and was one of the earliest leaders of the African American community there.

Although some black Canadian settlers left Nova Scotia for Sierra Leone in Africa in 1792 and 1800, those who remained welcomed immigrants, like Noah, who were seeking sanctuary from slavery.

With thanks to . . .

The Reverend Richard Belser of Saint Michael's Episcopal Church in Charleston for allowing me to follow Michael's footsteps through that historic church;

Walter Rhett and Ann Colwell, who walked the streets of Charleston with me and shared their expertise and thoughts about the relationships between black and white Charlestonians during the early nineteenth century;

Harlan Greene and Sharon Cruz-Reidbord of the Charleston County Public Library, and Roger Duncan, author of Coastal Maine: A Maritime History, who read sections of this manuscript and, with their special knowledge and insight, helped me to recreate scenes of 1804 to 1807. Of course, any remaining errors are fully my responsibility.

Bibliography

Note: Hundreds of sources, both primary and secondary, were used as background for writing Seaward Born. This list includes only some of the sources relevant to understanding the world of early-nineteenth-century African Americans in Charleston and in the other cities and towns related to this story. An excellent introduction to this topic written for young people is *The Young Oxford History of African Americans*, a multivolume series published by Oxford University Press.

Berlin, Ira. *Many Thousands Gone: The First Two Centuries of Slavery in North America*. Cambridge, Mass.: Harvard University Press, Belknap Press, 1998.

Blassingame, John W., ed. *Slave Testimony: Two Centuries of Letters, Speeches, Interviews and Autobiographies*. Baton Rouge: Louisiana State University Press, 1977.

Bolster, W. Jeffrey. *Black Jacks: African American Seamen in the Age of Sail*. Cambridge, Mass.: Harvard University Press, 1997.

Botkin, B. A., ed. *Lay My Burden Down: A Folk History of Slavery*. Chicago: University of Chicago Press, Phoenix Books, 1945.

Coker, P. C. III. *Charleston's Maritime Heritage, 1670-1865*. Charleston: CokerCraft Press, 1987.

Courlander, Harold. *A Treasury of Afro-American Folklore: The Oral Literature, Traditions, Recollections, Legends, Tales, Songs, Religious Beliefs, Customs, Sayings, and Humor of Peoples of African Descent in the Americas*. New York: Marlowe, 1976.

Curtin, Philip D. ed. *Africa Remembered: Narratives by West Africans from the Era of the Slave Trade*. Madison, Wis.: University of Wisconsin Press, 1968.

Ferguson, Leland. *Uncommon Ground: Archaeology and Early African America, 1650-1800*. Washington, D.C.: Smithsonian Institution Press, 1992.

Franklin, John Hope, and Loren Schweninger. *Runaway Slaves: Rebels on the Plantation*. New York: Oxford University Press, 1999.

Fraser, Walter J., Jr. *Charleston! Charleston! The History of a Southern City*. Columbia, S.C.: University of South Carolina Press, 1989.

Genovese, Eugene D. *Roll, Jordan, Roll: The World the Slaves Made*. New York: Pantheon Books, 1972.

Hess, Karen. *The Carolina Rice Kitchen: The African Connection*. Columbia, S.C.: University of South Carolina Press, 1992.

Horton, James Oliver and Lois E. Horton, *In Hope of Liberty: Culture, Community and Protest Among Northern Free Blacks, 1700-1860*. New York: Oxford University Press, 1997.

Hurmence, Belinda, ed. *Before Freedom, When I Can Just Remember: Twenty-seven Oral Histories of Former South Carolina Slaves*. Winston-Salem, N.C.: John F. Blair, 1989.

Joyner, Charles. *Down by the Riverside: A South Carolina Slave Community*. Chicago: University of Illinois Press, 1984.

Kolchin, Peter. *American Slavery, 1619-1877*. New York: Hill and Wang, 1993.

Littlefield, Daniel C. *Rice and Slaves: Ethnicity and the Slave Trade in Colonial South Carolina*. Chicago: University of Illinois Press, 1981.

Morgan, Philip D. *Slave Counterpoint: Black Culture in the Eighteenth-Century Chesapeake and Lowcountry*. Chapel Hill, N.C.: University of North Carolina Press, published for the Omohundro Institute of Early American History and Culture, 1998.

Pachai, Bridglal. *Peoples of the Maritimes: Blacks*. Halifax, Canada: Nimbus Publishing, 1997.

Piersen, William D. *Black Yankees: The Development of an Afro-American Subculture in Eighteenth-Century New England*. Amherst, Mass.: The University of Massachusetts Press, 1988.

Pope-Hennessy, James. *Sins of the Fathers: A Study of the Atlantic Slave Traders, 1441-1807*. New York: Alfred A. Knopf, 1968.

Taylor, Yuval, ed. *I Was Born a Slave: An Anthology of Classic Slave Narratives*. Vol. 1.: 1772-1849. Chicago: Chicago Review Press, Lawrence Hill Books, 1999.

Wade, Richard C. *Slavery in the Cities: The South, 1820-1860*. New York: Oxford University Press, 1964.

Wood, Peter H. *Black Majority: Negroes in Colonial South Carolina from 1670 Through the Stono Rebellion*. New York: W. W. Norton, 1974.